BUDDHIST
FOLK TALES

BUDDHIST
FOLK TALES

KEVIN WALKER

The
History
Press

In a world where you can be anything, be kind.

Unknown

First published 2022

The History Press
97 St George's Place, Cheltenham,
Gloucestershire, GL50 3QB
www.thehistorypress.co.uk
© Kevin Walker, 2022

British Library Cataloguing in Publication Data.
A catalogue record for this book is available from the British Library.

ISBN 978 0 7509 9865 9

Typesetting and origination by The History Press
Printed and bound in Great Britain by TJ Books Limited.

CONTENTS

THE STORY SO FAR: AN INTRODUCTION

Back in the early 1980s, I moved to a slightly different area of Yorkshire and, in my excursions to discover new delights, I came across a recently refurbished Victorian arcade. It was filled with enticing shops, a café, tattoo place and various independent businesses. One of the shops that caught my eye was a 'One World Shop'. A large, bright and beautifully displayed window was filled with wonders: artefacts, pieces of art and furniture, and clothes, all ethically sourced from around the world – something quite new for the town.

Amongst the wonders was a marvellous, seated statue of Buddha. It was so serene and elegant, and made even more noticeable by the fact it was the purest white in colour. It was not expensive, but I had just moved to a new house, so I didn't buy it. That was a dreadful mistake. I worried about it all week – why hadn't I just bought it when I saw it?

Two weeks later I went back to the shop and … it was still there! I can remember the feeling of joy as the shop-keeper wrapped it in white tissue paper and placed it safely in a rough, cardboard box. I went home with my treasure and placed 'him' on the windowsill of the wide staircase.

The first of many. Perhaps an unconventional introduction to Buddhism, but an important step in my interest in this most fascinating of belief systems.

Over the years since then, not only has my collection of images of the Buddha grown, but so has my knowledge of the concepts of his teachings. I have many books, have visited Buddhist sites in Britain and have travelled far and wide in the world to temples, monasteries and places of significance. I regularly attended weekly teaching and meditation sessions at an intriguing temple close by, as well as several retreats. My interest has helped me through some of the darkest times in my life and I even considered joining an order at one time. As an oral, performance storyteller, I developed an evening of Buddhist tales that I performed around the country, and some of these tales have now morphed into this collection of stories. I have written them not only during the difficult time of Covid, but also during a couple of personal health scares. At times I was in a deep state of inertia, as many were, and found that I could neither write nor paint, but as I became more accustomed to the situation, I started creating again, and I found researching and writing these stories uplifting and rewarding.

The stories in this collection, are, in the main, ancient. Most are taken from the Jataka tales – a huge collection of stories attributed to Buddha himself. They were originally written in Pali, an early language, and are a group of stories that tell of Buddha's pre-lives before he was born as the Buddha we recognise today – in other words, before his 'enlightenment'. They are regarded as folk tales, even though they are about such a venerated figure. This is mainly because they contain speaking animals, a little magic, journeys and decisions, morals to consider, and, of course, have been told, listened to, studied and used in teaching for over two and a half millennia. We do not know the authors of any of these stories and so I pay homage now to those wise and creative writers before me. I do not read Pali and therefore have used a collection of sources for the stories, which I have retold in my own style. I have listed these sources at the end of the book, and I thank all the translators and authors who put in the initial hard work for me. (I found Robert Chalmers's 1895 edition of the tales (Cambridge: University Press) to be the most useful.)

The Jataka tales is a vast collection of stories – 547 in all. Back in 2007, I travelled to Sri Lanka on my own to visit some of the temples and sites on this Buddhist island. I was staggered by the beauty of the land and the kindness of the people I met, but also by the poverty and the injustices of the area. I spent some time in the centre of the country in the city of Kandy – a hotspot of temples. It was truly magnificent, an experience that will live with me forever. I stayed in a large Victorian hotel that had a faded and genteel style. There was a wonderful lake nearby that was great to walk around in the evening. Along its banks were beautiful buildings; some of them were schools with hordes of uniformed and excited children of all ages, others were private houses, and one was a famous book shop. All my guides said I must visit the shop. I found it and looked at the comprehensive collection of books on every aspect of Buddhism, but I had difficulty finding what I was looking for, and here my naivety shone.

I was looking for a book of children's stories, stories I hoped to add to my storytelling in schools; I thought it was called 'The Jakarta Tales'. I was on my own, so a little anxious because of the language and the currency. Fortunately, the shop owner spoke perfect English and listened whilst I described what I was looking for. 'You want the whole collection?' he asked. 'If that is possible,' I answered. He disappeared and after a while reappeared carrying a huge box packed tightly with a series of shiny, hardback books. I nearly passed out at the sight of them. Not only would they obviously cost a fortune but how would I continue my travels and then get them back on the plane? I think I kept my cool, extracted just one to leaf through and then, to my shame, said that I would think about it and return later in the week. I scuttled out of the shop. Not only had I been expecting a compendium of stories that would fit in one nice book, like Grimm's fairy tales can sometimes do, but I had called them 'The Jakarta tales' instead of 'The Jataka tales', making sense of a new word in my very English way. I still go hot thinking about it.

The Jataka tales are, quite rightly, highly regarded in many Eastern countries. They are fun, scary, surprising, shocking, contemplative and educational, and, of course, over the centuries, the stories and their themes have spread to other areas, probably taken by merchants or armies who heard them being told on their travels. Some of Aesop's tales bear a striking resemblance to the tales, and it is thought that the troops of Alexander the Great's army may have carried them back to Greece. Their themes arise in European fairy tales, too. Jataka 206 bears a resemblance to The Lion and the Mouse, 322 to Chicken Licken, 380 to Rumpelstiltskin and there are various tales that use the image of the golden goose. They are also found in tales from Persia and areas of the continent of Africa, as well as in Hinduism and Judaism.

I have included two stories in the collection that would be considered more sensitive than the usual folk tale: the first is 'It Started with a Dream' and the second is 'The Walking Stick'. One is the account of the birth of Buddha and the other is about the death of the thirteenth Dalai Lama and the subsequent search for the current Dalai Lama. I do hope that you will forgive me placing these two stories amongst a group of folk tales. They are beautiful stories and do contain many of the elements of a folk tale. I included them both in my performance and they were well received. They are both also wonderful in demonstrating certain concepts in Buddhism. The birth of the Buddha is a lyrical story and contains spiritual images combined with historical comments. The story of the Dalai Lama is complicated and fascinating. Both stories deal with the idea of reincarnation and what happens after death, an important concept in Buddhism.

In Buddhism, one is encouraged to live a good life as set down in the precepts of whichever form of Buddhism one follows. Living a good life obviously is beneficial to this life, for everyone concerned, but it also has a 'knock-on' effect on our next life. Buddhists strive to reach Nirvana. This is a state of purity, nothingness and peace, where at last the shackles of this world are thrown off, a state much desired. Our current life has a huge effect on our next life and our 'climb' upwards towards Nirvana. The majority of Buddhists are not reincarnated as a new being when they die. Instead, this life influences the next life, as in cause and effect. The best explanation I was given was by using a snooker analogy. When a player hits the white ball towards, say, the blue ball, the blue ball will move forward in some way. That does not mean the white ball becomes the blue ball, but the way the white ball strikes the blue directly influences the way the blue ball moves onwards. A sharp, hard collision may make the blue ball crash forward or spin to one side if not hit centrally. If there is a gentle tap, the blue ball will also move on gently. And, of course, the aim of the game is to reach the pockets. Sometimes the blue ball will go straight in, sometimes just miss, perhaps causing difficulty for the next shot, and sometimes something drastic happens: it flies off the table. So, with life. It can be a long game to reach the end. Hopefully, the time will come, and one will reach that blessed state of Nirvana, or Enlightenment. Some holy individuals, who see that they have much more to carry out on this earth to help others, can choose to return to the earth as another human, rather than moving on to Nirvana; hence, reincarnation for some. The Blessed Dalai Lama has chosen this path, and when he dies, it means that within a short time – a few years – a child will be born who is the incarnate being of the former Dalai Lama and must be found by various, well-trodden means. Again, forgive my layman talk. But both 'It Started with a Dream' and 'The Walking Stick' involve elements of this.

The Jataka tales are mainly stories about animals and people that are the various past lives of Buddha as he made his way towards Enlightenment, and 'It Started with a Dream' is the beginning of the story of the last life of Buddha on earth. I have included only the story of his birth but, of course, his last life on earth is filled with remarkable stories of his long life and how he finally reached Enlightenment. I would encourage you to read further stories. In southern Spain, high in the hills above the commercial Costa Del Sol town of Benalmadena, there is the most beautiful, modern Stupa, a Buddhist temple, in the shape of a lotus. Inside, you find colourful murals of various aspects of the Buddha's life painted high on the walls above you. It is truly a magical place to visit. It stands on a carved plateau, overlooking the town and the Mediterranean Sea, a huge stylised white and gold building, incongruous in many ways with the hotels and beach bars down below.

Another story I have included is an original tale that has arisen from much reading and discussion regarding the lost years of Jesus and a possible different ending from the established story. It is followed by research notes and conclusions. I offer it respectfully as an interesting line of thought to contemplate. I have never told this story; in fact, I have never before completed the story by putting all the 'facts' into story form, but during my performance, I offered forward all the lines of research and loosely suggested the narrative of the story, much to the interest of the listeners. I offer them now to you as a completed story to ruminate upon.

I have many happy memories of performing 'It Started with a Dream' around the country. I usually set up a backdrop of Buddhist artefacts and statues of Buddha, but one time I was flying in from Spain to perform and I could only bring one Buddha with me. So, well before the performance, I explained to the prospective audience my dilemma, and suggested, if they wish, they bring a Buddha image with them to put on the stage. I was amazed at how many were brought into the marquee in the hours before the performance was due to take place. Each one was beautifully 'wrapped', so precious, and many had the most beautiful stories attached to them – how old they were, someone special they had belonged to, some distant land they came from. I had, of course, promised to look after the images with great care. Before the performance, I began to arrange them, draping gorgeous cloths and trying to give each one prominence. As I was doing this, a young lad appeared by my side to watch. It was a festival and at the other side of the site was a circus skills training marquee, and children could borrow various items of circus equipment to practise with. Yes, you've guessed it – he had borrowed some of the said equipment! A long, colourful ribbon, on the end of a springy stick, to wave around and make beautiful shapes with. And now he began to make those beautiful shapes – well, actually, he was having difficulty controlling the long ribbon, and here he was, right next to those precious, loaned, images. I had to use every skill I had as an adult, ex-teacher and a performer with pre-performance nerves to gently persuade him to prac-tise outside the marquee.

So, my journey with Buddhism carries onward.

And the elegant, white statue of Buddha I talked about? I now have a huge collection spread out through the house and garden and presently limit myself to what I collect. They all mean so much to me and each carries its own story and significance. When I moved away to live in Spain, I left one of my favourite wooden Buddhas, bought in Indonesia, with a great friend of mine, to 'look after' for me, a point of contact between us. She has kept it all these years, and it now sits in the home she lives in. She has a five-year-old grandson who comes to stay and when he is there he always adorns the Buddha with flowers, jewellery or other trinkets, and she sends me photos that make me smile. This elegant wooden Buddha is obviously having the same effect on Max.

The white Buddha sits on a shelf in my little garden studio, above where I work at my painting and writing. I often smile to myself when I think back to buying him, how I was so pleased that he was still there in the shop window when I returned. I never thought at the time that the likelihood was that he was not the original I had spotted two weeks before, that several could have been sold in that time and replaced from stock; he is a simple plaster of Paris image covered in gloss paint. He is faded now, almost cream, and bears the marks and knocks of many house moves, but he is still there, a constant in my life. A symbol of my Buddhist beliefs.

I hope you enjoy these tales. A collection of stories that mean a great deal to me. Stories of old Buddhism covering difficult topics; enduring Buddhism; and stories that have such meaning for now and the future.

1

WILD
STRAWBERRIES

A story that is told in many cultures and derives from the Jataka collection.

There was a man hurtling down a jungle path, running as fast as he could, continually looking over his shoulder in desperation, for he was being pursued by a huge, fierce tiger, hungry for its next meal. Suddenly, his escape route was halted by a wide chasm that opened before him, the cliff sides falling steeply to a distant rocky floor. What was he to do? Gathering all his strength, he took a few steps backwards, ran forwards and leapt with all his might, hoping to land safely on the other side. But his leap was not far enough and, to his horror, he plummeted downwards, yelling as he fell. Fortunately, there was a strong vine growing out of one side of the chasm and he managed to grab it and stop his fall. And so there he was, heart thumping loudly, gasping for breath and gently swaying in the void. He looked up and saw the furious tiger growling down at him, and when he looked down, to his horror, he saw the tiger's mate growling up at him.

As he clung to the vine wondering what would happen next, he heard a strange noise. Just beyond his grip on the vine … a jungle mouse was gnawing through the precious vine.

He sighed a heavy sigh.

Looking straight ahead, he saw some wild strawberries growing on a ledge on the chasm's cliff wall. He reached out and plucked the juiciest fruit he could reach and ate it. And in that moment, he thought it was the sweetest strawberry he had ever tasted.

2

THE TALKATIVE
TURTLE

(JATAKA 215)

This is a story I have been telling for many years and it is a tale that again has been adopted by several cultures.

Amongst the ponds and inlets and squishy places, there lived a turtle. He lived by himself and enjoyed swimming in his water and climbing in and out to sunbathe on the bank. He also liked to talk. To anyone, and sometimes to no one. He loved endless chatter. He was an expert on the weather, the coolest water, the best places to feed, in fact anything you cared to mention. And I am afraid the other creatures of the waterways found him more than a little boring. As he walked or swam along, chuntering to himself, the other animals and birds would fling themselves into bushes, take flight or dive deep into the murky depths in order to avoid holding a conversation with him. He was quite lonely but made the best of life.

One day he was slowly making his way down the pathway, talking away to himself, when he heard wonderful chattering and laughter high above him in the trees. It was difficult for him to look up, so he backed away, then stretched his patterned neck and head skyward. High above him was a gathering flock of birds, each one twittering away in excitement.

'Hello,' shouted the turtle, 'You all sound excited, what is happening?'

The birds gradually settled and looked around to see where the voice was coming from.

'Oh, it's you, Turtle,' said one of them, and they all began to giggle, ready for one of his long conversations. Two birds flew down to him. It was a good day for them, so they were quite happy to chat – well, listen.

'Today is the day we all take flight and fly to the other side of the world where the food is plentiful, and we can make our nests and raise our families.'

'Oh, that does sound exciting,' said the turtle, feeling sad that he couldn't travel more like them. 'I wish I could come with you,' he added despondently.

The whole flock of birds squawked with laughter. 'You, how could you come with us? You don't have wings!'

The turtle pulled his head in a little, he felt embarrassed. But then, feeling braver, his head came out fully and he shouted, 'Where there is a will, there is a way. Let me think!'

This time he pulled his head in fully, and in the dark shell, he scrunched up his eyes and thought hard. Suddenly, his head popped out, his eyes shining brightly: 'I have it!'

All the birds went silent as they listened to his plan. 'Yes, I have it. It's simple really. I will find a stick and two of you strong birds can hold each end of the stick in your beaks, then I will hold on tight in the middle. You two, *strong* birds can then flap your wings and take off, taking me with you.'

'But is your mouth strong enough to hold on?' asked one bird. 'More to the point, can you keep your mouth closed long enough, during the long flight?' added another.

Again, all the birds laughed. They knew how much the turtle liked to talk and how difficult he would find it, not being able to chat whilst they travelled.

The turtle looked hurt. 'Of course my jaws are strong enough, and I can promise you, I can be the quietest creature around the pond … when I care to be.'

All the birds shrugged. 'Very well,' they said, 'but we cannot guarantee your safety, that has to be your job.'

The turtle looked around and saw a nice dry stick lying on the ground not far from him. He gave it a little wipe, and, taking a big breath, grasped the middle of the stick with his strong jaws. Two of the larger birds flew down and, just before grabbing the stick, one asked, 'You ready?'

The turtle was just about to answer 'yes', with a long explanation as to why he was ready, when he realised it was a test, and he simply nodded his head instead. The two birds raised their eyebrows at him, but nevertheless, they took hold of the ends of the stick. With much flapping of wings, the two strong birds took off from the ground, with the turtle hanging between them. The other birds screeched loudly, took flight, and the flock began to circle the pond before heading off to the other side of the world … with their strange companion.

As they flew around in a large circle, there were two children watching them down on the ground. 'Oh, look how wonderful the birds are, I bet they are flying to somewhere far away!' shouted one of them, and the turtle shook with excitement at the thought.

'But what is that in the middle? Is it a turtle?' asked the other. 'That can't be a turtle flying with them?'

'Oh yes, it is. How clever of the birds to carry a turtle like that! Fancy them thinking of an idea like that.'

The turtle gave a shudder of annoyance. How clever of them? It was *my* idea, not the birds'.

'Have a wonderful journey you clever birds!' both children shouted.

This was too much for the turtle. 'It was my ideaaaaaaaaaaaaa …!'

Amongst the ponds and inlets and squishy places, there lived a turtle. He lived by himself and enjoyed swimming in his water and climbing in and out to sunbathe on the bank. He also liked to talk, especially of the time he flew with the birds.

3

MAYBE

This short and well-known story is a delight. I am sure that you could continue its theme for a few more lines.

High up in the mountains, just below the snow line, there was a farmer who had worked in the fields all his life, making a good but simple life for him and his family. One day, his prize horse bolted away out of sight. When they heard the news, neighbouring farmers came to give their condolences. 'What bad luck,' they all said in various ways.

'Maybe,' said the old farmer.

Next morning, the horse had made his way home, bringing three wild horses with him. 'How wonderful!' the neighbours said.

'Maybe,' answered the farmer.

The next day, the farmer's oldest son tried to ride one of the magnificent wild horses. Try as he might, the wild horse would not be tamed, and it threw the farmer's son to the ground and broke his leg. The son was the main worker on the farm, and the neighbours once again came to give their sympathy. 'What dreadful bad luck,' they all said.

'Maybe,' replied the farmer.

The following day, the military came riding into the village, looking for strong young men to draft into the army. When they saw the broken leg of the farmer's son, of course they passed him by. The neighbours congratulated the old farmer on how well things had turned out.

'Maybe,' said the farmer.

4

A Favourite Tree

When I walk in the countryside or even around the suburb where I live, I always keep an eye on the trees. Are they in blossom? When will their leaves burst forth, their shape, their bare form?

Deep in the forest there lived an antelope. He spent his time in the sunshine clearings eating grass, or deep in the shady scrubland keeping safe. He looked out for trees when they were in full fruit and would gather their sweet offerings as they fell to the ground. There was one mighty tree that had become his favourite. In its wide branches, the fruits were abundant and fell to the ground over many weeks. The antelope spent much time there.

But into the forest came a hunter. He captured and killed antelopes and deer for a living. He would place fruits under a tree, climb into its branches and dangle a rope trap around the fruits on the ground – a sort of noose. Then, he would wait for his prey to step into the noose.

Early in the morning, the hunter was in the forest and had set up his trap under the antelope's favourite tree, spreading delicious fruits on the ground to tempt any passing animals to stop and eat.

The antelope approached the tree and stopped for a while; he was always on the lookout for danger. He saw the abundance of fruits lying on the floor and wondered why there were so many, and why hadn't some been eaten by the night-time animals? He was afraid that something could be wrong.

The hunter, hiding in the branches of the tree, saw the antelope approaching but was worried when the animal stopped, as if it had sensed danger. Anxious that it might run off, the hunter began throwing fruit from the tree towards the antelope, trying to tempt the creature closer. But this antelope was a wise creature. He knew that fruits on a tree only fell straight down to the ground. These were flying towards him and he knew this meant danger. He looked very carefully into the branches of the tree and spotted the hunter hiding there. However, he pretended not to see him.

The antelope raised his head and said out loud, 'My good friend the magnificent fruit tree, you used to feed me well by dropping your fruits to the ground so I could eat them, but now you are throwing them at me! You seem to have changed your habits so I will change mine, too. I will go and eat fruit from a tree that is still acting like a tree!'

The hunter was furious when he realised that he had been outsmarted by the antelope and he shouted, 'You might have escaped me this time clever antelope, but don't you worry, I shall catch you next time for sure!'

The antelope smiled to himself. The hunter had given himself away again with his anger. 'Oh, I am sad my friend the tree. Now, you don't sound anything like a tree. In fact, you sound like a hunter, a human hunter, too. I am glad that I am a peace-loving creature who never kills anything to eat. I am far wiser than you will ever be. I am not harming anything in this life nor condemning myself in future lives. Whilst you? … Well, I feel pity for you.'

And with that, he gambolled off into the forest, leaving behind a bemused hunter, foolishly sitting in his tree.

MUDDIED WATER

The Buddha and his disciples were journeying across the land. They had travelled far and were soon to cross a wide desert. They stopped and camped by some caves, and, in the distance, they could see a lake. The Buddha called to him his youngest follower, an eager young man who had much enthusiasm and much to learn. The Buddha asked him to go down to the lake and collect water for the group.

The young man was always eager to carry out the Buddha's wishes, and taking two large jars he made his way down to the lake. When he got there, he could only find one place to access the water. It was near where a river flowed into the lake, next to a crossing ford. The water was crystal clear. He made his way down to the water's edge and was just about to dip his jar into the water, when an ox cart appeared and crossed the river using the nearby ford. To the frustration of the man, the water was suddenly muddy and clouded, caused by the oxen's hooves and the carriage wheels.

'There is no way we can drink this water now,' he said, and he gathered up the empty jars and made his way back to the camp.

'The water was stirred by a crossing oxen and cart, there was no way I could bring you that muddy water to drink,' explained the young man to his teacher.

The Buddha said nothing, but about half an hour later asked if the young man could once again go down and collect some water. The young man cheerfully collected the jars and walked down to the same place, but the water was still muddy and cloudy, and so he came back with empty jars once again.

'The water is still undrinkable. I think we should find a local town and find water there.' But the Buddha said nothing.

Again, about an hour later, the Buddha asked once more if the young man could go and fetch water from the lake. The young man was happy to carry out the Buddha's wishes, but inside he was angry, as he knew that the water would still be muddy and undrinkable.

But when he reached the lake, he discovered that it was now crystal clear. He carefully lowered each jar into the water, filling them with cooling drinkable water, and carried them back to camp. He placed them in front of the Buddha, who asked, 'What did you do to make the water clean?'

The young man was confused – it was obvious that he had done nothing.

The Buddha looked at him and explained, 'You waited and let it be. Therefore, the mud settled, and the water became clear. Sometimes our mind is like that, too. When it is muddy, we must give it time. We must be patient. It will reach a balance by itself without having to try to calm it down. Everything will pass on its own as long as you don't hold on to it.'

THE KING AND THE TORTOISE

(JATAKA 345)

A simple tale that reminds me of the Aesop's Fable, 'The Hare and the Tortoise'.

The king of Benares was a kind and thoughtful ruler, but of late he had become lazy, even indolent, preferring to laze around rather than govern his country and lead by example. One of his chief ministers became concerned about his master's new disposition and wondered how he could best help.

One day, the two of them were out walking in the palace gardens. The minister had persuaded the king to go there to talk over policy, and to encourage him to take at least *some* exercise. Whilst they were walking and talking, the king looked down and saw a tortoise, slowly ambling along.

'What is that?' asked the king, for he had never seen one before.

'Oh, that is a tortoise, sire. It is a creature that can be walking almost every hour in the day, and yet not get far. Some call him lazy.'

The minister called to the tortoise. 'Hey, Sir Waddler, you move so slowly! I wonder what would happen to you if suddenly there was a fire that moved swiftly across the palace garden? How would you survive?'

The tortoise stopped for a moment and looked up. 'I may seem to be moving slowly, and some call me lazy, but I am always on the move and alert, and know all the holes and hide-away places wherein I could climb and therefore be safe. If *I* didn't survive, none of us would.'

'You see how wise this fellow is, sire? One that keeps moving, resting when he needs to, but is always alert to what is happening around him, making great strides in the world. More so than the one who rushes only when he needs to and lounges the rest of the time.'

The king nodded at the wise words, and from then on changed his ways.

THE NEW BUDDHA

Many years ago, I was invited to spend a few days with a walking group in southern Spain, telling them stories during the walks and in the evenings. One day, we hiked up the Alpujarras Mountains to a most magical Buddhist monastery. As we approached the main buildings, we could see a new statue that had been erected in the middle of a large pond. Signs of heavy machinery could still be seen in the disturbed grass and mud, from the difficult task of placing the statue in the perfect place. The group sat on the grass, and I told them this story. It was quite a magical experience.

The students pulled their saffron robes around them to keep out the chill, as they rushed through the hallways of the monastery to the large central meeting room. It was not very often that they were all summoned to a meeting at once – it usually meant some special news or announcement. They all settled on the floor and at last the chief monk stepped before them. One hundred and fifty dedicated students.

Their leader welcomed them as usual and then at last launched into his news. The monks had decided to set the students an unusual task. They were to be sent out into the world for six months to help raise enough gold and silver to create a new statue of the Buddha. There was an audible gasp from the students, and much chatter. Their master quietened them and explained in more detail. It was felt that this current intake of students was of the highest quality and their teachers wanted to mark this by installing a new statue of the Buddha, but a statue provided by the students themselves. They were not to beg for the precious metals – no, they were to earn them. In exactly six months, they must return to the monastery with whatever they had collected. It would be weighed and assessed, and the monastery craftsmen would make a mould so that the metals could be melted down and poured into it, creating a special image for the prayer room. They must decide carefully how they should earn this collection of precious metals, choosing which of their many talents they should employ in the outside world. He wished them well and sent them out on their mission, reminding them to return in exactly six months' time.

The assembled students bowed to their teachers and then scurried off back to their dormitories to collect their few possessions. There was much talk and laughter, as all were excited by the task. The chance to create a new statue dedicated to their intake … but also the chance to be out in the world for six whole months. Of course, some were anxious. How would they survive on their own? But most relished the prospect.

They left the confines of the monastery, wished each other farewell and good luck, and disappeared down the mountain paths towards the myriad of little villages and hamlets, plans buzzing in their heads. Some had decided to try teaching in the poorer communities, working in the hospitals or farming the land; each hoped their chosen path would earn them their prize.

One young man sat beneath a tree in the cool and thought. What could he offer over the next six months? It needed to be something that he was good at, but it also needed to be something that would earn him the most precious metals possible. You see, he had decided that he wanted to be the best, the most successful. He knew it was wrong to be proud but, oh, how he wished to collect the most gold and silver of all the students. He imagined the scene in six months' time when, to the amazement of the other students, he presented a huge bag of treasure to his teachers. Now, what was he good at? Storytelling. Of course! Many times, he had been left in charge of a group of students to tell them stories from the life of the Buddha. He somehow could remember all the details, and they were entranced by the way he told them. But he also told stories that made his friends laugh, or scared them in the dark.

And so he set off to the nearest little town. He found a set of stone steps in a busy part and began telling passing townsfolk that in one hour's time he would be telling wonderous stories that would entertain and amaze them. He was a little shy to begin with but soon gained confidence when he realised there was a genuine interest.

When the allotted time arrived, there was quite a crowd sitting on the steps and on the floor in front of him. He introduced himself and explained what his mission was, emphasising the fact that it was gold and silver he was collecting, and why. One or two of the audience sidled away, knowing they would not be able to donate anything, and the young man made a mental note to mention next time that anyone could listen, there was no pressure to give to the collection. And so, he began. He imagined his friends back at the monastery, hanging on his every word as he told them Buddhist stories, scary stories, stories of the great and the foolish, even love stories, and this technique worked. The crowd laughed and jeered, silent at times but at others screaming in delight. More people gathered as the performance went on and, as he made one final flourish with a farewell bow, the audience stood and cheered. The young man placed his feeding bowl on the ground, and several people stepped forward to proudly place in it what they could afford. A man approached him and quietly asked him if he was free that evening to come up to the large house above the village to entertain some guests he had staying. Of course, he agreed.

The evening performance was quite different. Fewer were in the audience, but all lounged on large floor cushions with goblets of drink in their hands. And all were wearing the most beautiful gold and silver jewellery. He told his best stories and delighted everyone there. Even the servants could be seen peeping through the screens enjoying the fun. And the applause was loud and encouraging. He placed his bowl on the floor and the guests happily searched in their purses for suitable coins or removed pieces of jewellery, placing them in the bowl. The owner was so pleased with his performance that he offered him food and a place to sleep that night. He ate and slept well and departed next morning with a spring in his step.

And so the next six months progressed well. He would stage a performance in a town during the day, to much applause, and every time some rich man would ask him to visit his home in the evening. Large and small towns, large and small great houses, too. And his bag of precious metals began to swell considerably – so much so, that he had to return to his own family's house to ask his father if he could store it there. His father was impressed by his son's success and gladly locked away the precious load in a strong cupboard.

The young man continued his progression around the local area, returning to his father's twice to store his collection. But then, the end of the six months came. The young man was sad in many ways – he had enjoyed his time and it was good to make his father proud – but, oh, he was so looking forward to his return to the monastery.

He planned his last day very carefully. He would head towards his father's house and perform one last time in the local town, carry on to his father's to pick up his treasure and then head swiftly back to the monastery. The last performance went well and he collected a last few gold and silver coins. He then rushed up to his father's farmstead, not intending to stay long, but giving himself plenty of time to journey back to the monastery with his heavy load. But when the young man arrived at his father's house, there was a surprise waiting for him. His father was so impressed by the success of his son's mission that he had organised one last performance for his friends and family, with even the servants allowed to watch from the sidelines. The young man was taken aback. He didn't really have the time, but when he saw the happy faces of his family and the wealth of the guests, he realised it was one last opportunity he couldn't miss.

The performance began, and although by now the young man was weary from his travelling and performing, he gave of his best, and the applause at the final bow was heartening, as was the look on his father's face. He looked at all the lamps ablaze and thought how late it was and how rushed his journey back through the night to the monastery would be. But his father insisted on telling the assembled guests just how well his son had done in tackling the task set by the good monks at the monastery, how hard he was working to become a good monk himself, and how important it was that everyone dug deep in their pockets to help with the collection. The young man was getting restless. He watched as his bowl was slowly passed around the family and friends, and gold and silver items were ceremoniously placed in it. It was presented to him, and he made as big a gesture as he could, pouring the collection into a by now huge saddle bag. His father wanted him to stay the night, to meet the guests and thank them individually, but the young man was by now quite frantic to make his escape to journey back to the monastery. He made his excuses, waved to the guests and shouted his thanks, prostrated to his parents and then hurried through the large kitchen to the back door.

But his escape was interrupted by his old nurse. She threw her arms around him and told him how proud she was of him, how he was going to make a great monk. She fell to the ground, prostrating herself to him. His nurse meant the world to him and he couldn't have her, of all people, behaving like this, so he helped her up. She grabbed his wrist and said, 'Oh my boy – oh yes, I still think of you as my boy, and I will always call you that, even when you become a great teacher. I would like to give something towards your collection.'

She began to fumble for her little purse and took so much time that the young man became angry at the delay, especially when she produced from her purse a small, copper coin.

'I am sorry, but I have to hurry. It is wonderful to see you but I am afraid I must get going … and your coin … it's not gold or silver, that is all I am collecting. Farewell!'

And he hurried off, leaving the old woman, arm extended, with her precious copper coin in her gnarled grip.

The journey was difficult. There was hardly any moon to give light, and the bag was heavy with its precious load.

But he travelled on, spurred on by the knowledge that his mission was almost over.

The morning sun rose over the mountains, but he had no time to appreciate its beauty. The monastery was in sight but still many miles away and he knew that the last part of the journey was a steep road.

At last, he made it. The monastery was buzzing with excitement. Everyone had arrived back over the last day or so, and all were eager for the gathering, where they could add their collected treasure to the communal heap. Everyone sat on the ground, some looking exhausted, and one by one they came out to the front and tipped their treasure, creating a gold and silver mountain on the tapestry rug. No matter whether the contribution was large or small, they were all equally praised by the onlookers. The young man was next, and he heaved his heavy bag forward. He made quite a show of loosening the ties, lifting the bag and pouring the enormous amount of treasure he had collected. There was a noticeable silence as the gold and silver poured onto the pile and then the students gathered their senses and gave their approval in the way they had done for all the other contributors. The young man's heart sank. He was expecting a cheer or at least some words from the chief monk, but no, the same approval as everyone else. He made his way back to his place. When everyone had given their contribution, then a loud cheer came, from everyone, for everyone.

The chief monk explained what would happen next. The craftsmen would assess the quantity of precious metals. They would make a wax model of the statue they had designed to the size that would equal the amount of metal.

A mould would be made, using the wax model. Then the forge would take over. The workmen would melt down the gold and silver and pour the molten liquid into the mould, the wax being burnt away by the heat. After many days of cooling, the mould would be peeled away, revealing the statue in all its glory.

The students listened with intense interest, inside disappointed that it would obviously be weeks before their hard work would be revealed, but patience was a virtue.

And the work began.

Smaller groups of students were invited to watch parts of the process. The craftsmen measuring the metal and calculating the size of the statue and the block of wax being slowly carved, with all its intricate details. The making of the mould, and the wax model being carefully placed inside the container and surrounded by fine sand. The metal workers at the forge, melting down the treasure to the correct temperature. The wonderful, honey-coloured liquid, carefully being poured into the mould, spluttering and bubbling with the heat burning away the wax. And then the wait.

Another week later, everyone gathered in the meeting hall again for the final reveal. The result of everyone's hard work. The now cool mould was placed on a heavy table, and everyone watched with bated breath as the mould was split open, almost violently, revealing the sand-covered form. By now, those at the back were standing; in front some were kneeling; others got to their feet and ran to the sides so they could have a better view. The artisans took stiff brushes and began to scrub away the sand from the surface; even they showed excitement on their faces as the image began slowly to be revealed. But then, everything suddenly halted. The craftsmen stood back, the monks rushed forward to look, and everyone gasped in horror. As the sand had been swept from the face of the image, it had become obvious that a huge fault had been left on the face, like a scar running from forehead to nose. There was utter silence, then much whispering between the artisans and, finally, explanatory utterances to the monks.

It was shocking, sad even, but something had simply gone wrong in the making process. It would have to be carried out again. And so, it was. Only this time, the students were not invited to watch any of the process so the artisans could concentrate fully on their work.

After many weeks of rigorous, concerted work on the part of the workmen, and much chanting and praying on the part of the students, all gathered once again in the meeting hall to watch the statue be released from its mould. There was silence in the hall as the workmen cracked open the mould casket, the hammer blows reverberating around the stone walls. Everyone held their breath as the statue was manhandled with care into position so the sand could once again be swept from the surface. All seemed to be going well, until, once again, the work came to a sudden halt and the craftsmen stood back in horror. The very same fault-line sliced across the statue's face causing the familiar scar from forehead to nose. The workmen shook their heads, the teachers looked perplexed, but the chief monk took charge and stepped forward to address the students.

'This is most troubling. Yet again, the face of the statue is scarred, and in the same place as before. This cannot have been due to negligence by the artisans and can only have been caused by ... you.' And he pointed at the students. There was silence as all waited for an explanation.

'I ask all of you to retire to your dormitories and think deeply. Is it you who is at fault? Did one of you beg for some of your contributions? Somehow falsely earn your share? Offend someone or even ... steal? Please, think deeply and come and tell me privately so that we can fix this worrying situation. Please leave now, in silence.'

The student monks stood quietly and returned to their dormitories to consider the situation. Some sat or lay on their beds, deep in thought. Others gathered in little groups, quietly discussing options. There were also a few raised voices.

The young storyteller sat on his bed and looked around at the others and was appalled that any of them should bring about such a dreadful thing because of their actions. He had worked so hard to earn his share. He had been honest with his audiences about his aspirations and had even allowed people to listen to his stories even if they couldn't afford to contribute. And he suddenly stopped his thoughts. Of course.

He wrapped his robes around him and left the monastery by the back door. He made his way down the mountain path to the little road that eventually led to his father's farmstead. His parents were surprised but pleased to see him again so soon, but he avoided their greetings and made his way to the kitchen. There he found his old nurse sitting by the cooking fire, stirring a pot. Her face lit up with delight when she saw him approaching her. She was about to stand to throw her arms around her young master, but before she could, he threw himself to the ground and prostrated himself before her.

'No, young master, no, please!'

The rest of the servants stood in disbelief as the young man lay before her and said, 'Yes, I must prostrate myself to the most wonderful and caring woman in the whole world, whom I wronged so dreadfully.'

'Shh, shhh, don't be silly, you have never wronged me.'

'Oh, but I have! In my pride and my haste to gather as much treasure as I could so my teachers and student colleagues would be impressed by my efforts, I wounded you greatly. After my storytelling I refused your offering of a hard-earned copper coin. If you could forgive me for my ignorance, and if you are still willing, I would gratefully accept your offering with all the joy in my heart.'

The old lady bent down and raised the young man to his knees. She found her little purse, rummaged around in it and dropped the little copper coin into his now grateful hand. He stood, kissed her forehead, thanked her, and turned and left.

Back at the monastery, word began to circulate the next day that the statue-making process had begun again. Theories were whispered and passed from one to another, but none of the students could truly find an answer to the dilemma.

After several weeks, the students were once again summoned to the great meeting hall, to watch the statue being liberated from its mould a third time. Hearts were in mouths as the sand was once again brushed away from the precious surface of the Buddha. And this time, well, the beams on the faces of the artisans said everything.

There, standing before the gathered students, craftsmen and their teachers was the most beautiful image of the Buddha. Elegant and serene and richly decorated with detailed designs.

And the face? Perfect. But what made this statue even more exquisite was the shape of a copper-coloured flame emblazoned on the forehead of the Buddha, a detail none of the craftsmen could explain, but only wonder at.

The chief monk smiled across at the young man, who nodded silently back to him.

And now, whenever the young man is left alone with a group of students, he still enchants them with stories of the life of the Buddha, stories of powerful men and foolish ones, and he always includes a new story, the story of 'The New Buddha'.

8

FRESH BREATH

Many years ago, in a lush part of India, there was a kingdom ruled by a young man called King Ashoka. He was a serious and pious ruler who believed in Buddhism and made great efforts to perform kind and good deeds, some of them too amazing to comprehend. Once he had his people build eighty thousand pagodas in one day. Many Buddhist masters visited his kingdom and he made offerings to them in their honour and listened intently to their teachings.

King Ashoka gave meals to local and visiting monks, and one day he noticed a young monk he had never met before. The man had a serious countenance but spoke well amongst his peers. He was obviously well learned. The king had just seated himself on the steps, amongst the monks, to eat food with them, when the new monk sat next to him. He was a quietly confident young master, at ease with himself. The king looked at his smiling face, ready to speak with the king, when Ashoka suddenly noticed a beautifully sweet, aromatic smell coming from the young man's mouth.

The king frowned a little, thinking, 'He must have something in his mouth creating this fragrance. Is he trying to deceive my people, disguising his ill-thought words with this pleasant smell?' And so, the king asked the young man to open his mouth. The king examined the inside of the monk's mouth, but he could find nothing hidden there. He gave the young man a tumbler of water and asked him to rinse out his mouth, which the young man happily did. But when he turned to the king, the sweet-smelling fragrance was still there.

At last, the king asked, 'Please tell me, young man. Why is there such a sweet-smelling aroma coming from your mouth? I have never smelled anything like it!'

'Your majesty, many years ago, in a previous life, I was a preacher at the time of the Buddha. I was a wise teacher, and many came to listen to my words. I happily praised the teachings of the Buddha and taught people how to live their lives well in the light of his teachings. From that time on, with every incarnation, this beautiful fragrance, not found in nature, has emanated on my breath, uplifting the hearts of anyone who smells it.'

The king was delighted at the young man's story and realised that there are many blessings available when praising the Buddha's teachings.

'There are, indeed, many blessings. Please listen to my words.'

And, as he spoke to the king, a group of listeners gathered around on the steps, delighted by the young monk's sweet words.

There was silence amongst the gathered listeners when the young man finished and bowed his head. King Ashoka had reached a deeper understanding with his words. Fresh breath indeed.

9

THE MISER

The evening was perfect for sitting under the stars and admiring the full moon. There was a light breeze that cooled the skin after the heat of the day and the air was filled with the scent of jasmine. The old man sat on his favourite bench in the garden of his splendid house and smiled. He was rich … but also a lecher and a skinflint by nature. He had created everything around him, lusting for pleasure, but he hated parting with his money.

As he looked up at the pine cones in the tree above him, his nostrils caught the aroma of cooking, and suddenly he had an overwhelming desire for lamb. An idea popped into his head. He had thought of a clever way of eating as much lamb as he wanted, without paying for it, and without losing face.

His sons were sent for, and when they arrived in the garden, they found their father deep in prayer.

'Spirit of the tree, bless our house, continue to bless our house for eternity, bless our house.'

The sons were not used to finding their father in such a spiritual mood.

He turned to them and asked, 'Why are we so blessed as a family? I believe it is this ancient tree. I believe the spirit of the tree has blessed us because it is so grateful that it lives with us in our garden. We must pay homage to the tree and sacrifice to it whenever we can. Arrange it, my sons.'

The young men listened to their father's serious words and sprang into action. They slaughtered lambs and built a shrine to worship the spirit of the tree, and that night their father ate well on as much lamb as he wanted and felt most satisfied that his plan had worked.

The shrine was visited many times a year, and the greedy old man fed well on the meat that his sons provided for him.

But alas, the old man became even older as the years passed, and on the evening before he was due to die, now weak and gravely ill, he had a strange dream. He dreamed that a herd of sheep came into the beautiful garden, and the leader of the herd stepped forward and demanded the life of the old man. And so it was, that when he died, in his next life he came back as a lamb in the herd belonging to his sons.

When the next day of worship arrived, the sons chose the very same lamb to sacrifice that was their father's new incarnation. Only now did the old man recognise the wrongs of his life and in his heart he yelled out to his sons, 'My sons! Please listen to me! This pine tree is just an old pine tree, nothing special. I just wanted to satisfy my greedy appetite. Please don't keep repeating my wrongs again and again, otherwise we will never escape from our suffering.'

At the very moment that one of the sons picked up the lamb and flourished the razor-sharp butcher's knife, a monk was passing by, begging for alms. He shouted, 'Stop!'

The monk had divine powers. He guided the sons to look carefully at the innocent lamb and they realised the poor creature's previous incarnation.

They fell to their knees in tears, realising what had almost happened, and there and then, they swore an oath.

'From now on, we will never kill any living creature and only do good deeds to sow future fields of blessings.'

10

MOTHER LOVE

(JATAKA 455)

Splashing around in a lotus pool, high in the mountains, was a baby elephant, enjoying the coolness of the water during the midday heat. Mother elephant kept a close eye on him. She looked with love on her perfect child. He was pure white, with a face and feet the same hue as coral, a silvery trunk and the beginnings of fine, strong tusks.

The two spent every minute of the day together. She would reach high into the branches and pluck him the tastiest leaves and the sweetest fruits to eat. She would feed them to him and say, 'First you, then me.' She bathed him in the cool water, taking water into her trunk and squirting it over his body. He would copy her, taking water into his trunk, but then squirting it at his mother's face, his favourite game. So would begin fun and frolics between the two, splashing around in their pool.

Tired, they would lie together in the coolness of the mud, trunks curled tightly. Then, as evening came and the coolness was delightful, she would lie under the bushes and watch him play with the other baby elephants.

And as time passed, the young elephant grew and grew. He became taller than all the other elephants, a fine white bull-elephant with strong, white tusks. But, as he grew stronger, his mother grew old and weak. Her skin became rough and cracked and her tusks yellow and broken. Finally, she became blind. But her son stayed with her. He still squirted water over her, but gently now, and he caressed mud into her skin to soften it. He now reached up into the branches and plucked the finest leaves and sweetest fruits, and gently fed them to her, saying, 'First you, then me.' Their favourite time was lying in the squidgy mud together, trunks tightly curled.

In the cool evening, he would guide her into the safety of the bush undergrowth, and then he would go roaming with the other elephants.

One evening, a local king was in the forest hunting, and he saw the magnificent young, white elephant. 'I must capture him. I want to ride him in the palace processions.' And so his men crept up on the white elephant, and using ropes and nets they managed to catch him and subdue him. He was taken back to the palace where he was placed in the ornate stables, his back was covered with the finest of cloths and he was fed juicy fruits and the sweetest of river water.

But the young elephant would not eat or drink. His beautiful coral-coloured face was streaked with tears, and he became thinner and thinner. No one could understand why the elephant was in such distress until one day the king came to see him.

'Magnificent beast! I house you in a wonderful stable, adorn you with silks and jewels, feed you with the finest of fruits and sweet river water and yet you do not eat or drink. I fear that you will die!' said the king. 'What can I give you to please you?'

The elephant turned his tear-stained face to the king and said, 'Silks and jewels, food and sweet water do not make me happy. My blind old mother is alone in the forest and has no one to care for her. Even if I die, I will not eat or drink until I can give her some first.'

The king stood back in amazement. 'Never have I seen such kindness, even amongst human beings! This poor elephant should not be chained in a stable, he should be free.' And with this, the elephant was freed.

The elephant ran from the palace and made his way into the mountains to the lotus pool, looking everywhere for his mother. At last, he found her, lying in the mud beside the pool, so weak she could hardly move. He gently bathed her in the cool water. She looked up and asked, 'Is it raining?'

'No, it's your son. The king has released me, and I have returned to care for you.'

She slowly raised her head to look at him, and he gently squirted water on her eyes to clean away the mud and the tears, and a miracle happened – her sight returned.

The young elephant then reached up and plucked the finest leaves and the sweetest of fruits and gently fed them to her.

'First you, then me.'

11

THE WORM

In an idyllic monastery, high in the hills, there were two monks who had known each other ever since they joined the order as young children. They had grown up together, studied and carried out missions with each other, and as time had passed, they had grown old together. And then they died within a few months of each other. One of them was reborn in the heavenly realms and the other monk was reborn as a worm in a dung heap.

The one up in heaven was having a heavenly time, enjoying everything that heaven had to offer. But one day he began thinking of his old friend and wondering where he was now. And so, he searched all the heavenly realms, but no matter how hard he searched, he could not find him.

Next, he tried the realm of human beings, but no matter where he looked on earth, his friend was nowhere to be found.

He searched the animal realm, and then the insect realm, and at last he located him; he had been reborn as a worm in a dung heap.

'Oh dear,' he thought. 'I am going to rescue my friend. I am going down to earth to that dung heap, and I am going to bring my old friend back up here to the heavenly realms where he can enjoy everything that is offered, all the pleasures and the bliss of living in these wonderful realms.'

He descended to earth, and when he found the dung heap he shouted to his friend.

The little worm wriggled out and shouted, 'Who are you and what do you want?'

'I am your old friend! Remember, we used to be monks together in a past life and I have come to take you back to heaven with me where life is wonderful and blissful.'

'Go away, get lost!' shouted the worm in reply.

'But we used to be such good friends, and I want you to experience all the good things I have in heaven.' And he told the little worm about all the delights of living in the heavenly realms.

But the worm said, 'No thanks! I am more than happy living in my dung heap, thank you very much. Go away.'

The heavenly monk stroked his chin and thought, 'If I could just make a grab at his tail and catch him, I could take him to heaven, and he could see all the wonders for himself.'

So, he grabbed hold of the worm's tail and began to tug hard, but the harder he tugged, the harder the worm clung onto his dung heap, and in the end, he escaped and wriggled down into his heap. And as he wriggled further down into the heap, the heavenly monk ascended upwards towards heaven, two friends, separated in that life.

12

Choosing a Tree

(Jataka 74)

Another story comparable to one of Aesop's Fables.

A new king had ascended the throne of Benares and began to make changes to make his kingdom and its citizens safer. This even applied to the tree fairies. King Vessavaṇa asked them to choose which tree, plant, shrub, vine or flower they would like to make their home in.

One wise tree fairy had chosen a tree in the midst of a forest. He knew it would be safer to be surrounded by many other trees, plants, shrubs, vines and flowers, all intertwined to give strength. Many of the other fairies listened to his wise words and they, too, chose the forest as home. But some fairies thought differently. Why would they want to live deep in a forest where no one would see them? No, they chose big trees that stood in the village squares, or on the edge of towns or cities. Besides, if they were seen more, the offerings given by the people would be greater.

A few weeks later, a great storm came to the country. It blew in gales and tornadoes and shook everything it encountered. The fairies who lived in the lone trees laughed to begin with. Their huge trees had vast roots that grew deep into the ground, holding them sturdy. But this soon proved a problem. They stood so solidly against the blasts of the storm that their leaves and twigs were whipped so much they blew off, quickly followed by their branches, until, at last, the remaining trunks were lashed so hard and could not bend and so were uprooted from the earth, crashing to the ground.

Deep in the forest, all the trees and other shrubs and vines had grown into each other, giving strength with their tangled mesh, and were safe. The wind blew them hard, but it could not dislodge any of them, and instead it blew over and around the forest, leaving all unharmed.

When the storm had passed, the fairies from the uprooted trees gathered their families together and travelled out to the forest to ask if they could make their home there, too.

It is usually the lone tree, planted in a garden pot, that blows over in the wind.

13

THE NEED TO WIN

I love the way this poem and accompanying story work so well together.

When an archer is shooting for nothing, he has all his skill.
If he shoots for a brass buckle, he is already nervous.
If he shoots for a prize of gold, he goes blind or sees two targets.
He is out of his mind!

His skill has not changed, but the prize divides him.
He cares.
He thinks more of winning than shooting.
And the need to win drains him of his power.

Chuang Tzu

The king glowered down at the Captain of the Guard.

'The challenge has been thrown down. Summon before me your ten best archers.'

The Captain of the Guard bowed quickly, backed away out of the stateroom and made his way to the soldiers' quarters.

So, what was this challenge? A battle? A land grab?

No, it was an archery contest suggested by the young king of a neighbouring country in an attempt to encourage friendship. A contest that would be held in his palace grounds to which teams of archers from many countries were invited, with small bags of gold as prizes. A fun event.

But this was not merely a fun event for our king – no. If his country was to take part, then his men would win all the prizes. That was his way. Everything in his country had to be the best, the biggest, the richest or the most prized.

And so, next morning, the ten archers were assembled before the king, who barked his wishes at them. The men looked sidewards at each other as they made their way to the archery field, where the king had set himself a dais from which to watch and judge the men. They were all expert and, of course, easily hit the targets, but the king was furious that none of them was accurate enough to hit the very centre of the targets.

'Again!' he yelled, 'but this time I want, no, demand, perfection!'

He sat back as the men each selected a fine arrow from their quiver, took aim, and fired, and each one hit the very centre of their targets. They turned to their king with smiles on their faces, but instead of praise he again yelled at them.

'Now, again! But this time I want you to split your second arrow with your third.'

The men looked at each other and their captain, who shrugged to his men and indicated that they should at least try. And try they did. Many were extremely near but although they were hitting the very centre of their targets, none of them could split the target arrow.

The king did not even yell at them for their failure. He simply stood and furiously left the dais, leaving the men feeling utter failures.

And so, the search began. The king needed to find the best archers in the land. Proclamations were made, the Captain of the Guard was sent out to scour the land, and although many tried to impress the king with their skills, all failed, and of course it was the fault of the Captain of the Guard.

And so, the king took it on himself to search. He travelled the country on horseback, with a trusted group of soldiers and sportsmen. Many men and some women tried to fulfil the king's difficult criteria, but all fell short.

One day, after a particularly difficult and long journey to assess another group of failed archers, the king was returning to the palace, when the horses were suddenly halted at a field where an amazing sight appeared before them. Although the king was exasperated by the wasted day, he climbed down from his horse to take a closer look.

At the far end of the field was a large cart. On the cart were painted targets, and in the very centre of each target was a precisely placed arrow. The field was long, the targets varied, and every arrow was perfectly placed in the centre of each. The king's face lit up and he looked around to find who this noble archer could be.

Sitting on a log, eating an apple, was a farm worker. He stood as the king marched up to him, held his apple behind his back and made a bow mixed with a curtsy. After all, this was the king, no less.

The king demanded to know who had fired these arrows. The man's shoulders slumped and he slowly pointed to himself.

'You? You have fired each of these arrows?'

The man nodded, with a slightly puzzled look on his face, as if he had committed a crime.

'Prove it to me. Now!' snapped the king.

The poor fellow sprang into action. Well, I say sprang. Actually, he lumbered to get his bow and his bag of arrows.

'Notice that none of the arrows is off target,' said the king. 'This is exciting, at last.'

The man smiled at the king, again made a mixture of a bow and a curtsy, and then turned away and began to walk down to the cart at the other end of the field. The king and his lords watched as the man struggled to turn round the cart. As he did so, they noticed that another side had similar targets with arrows in the middle of them. The excitement was mounting. When the cart was fully turned with a blank side showing, the man turned, bowed again, and made his way back to the king and his men. He gingerly picked up his homemade bow, selected an arrow, like the others fletched with a multitude of coloured feathers, fitted it into his bow, and, to the amazement of the watching audience, fired off the arrow at the blank side of the cart. The arrow just managed to hit the cart. He did the same, five times ... having to move a little nearer the cart part way through the demonstration as he nearly missed it on the third shot.

When he had finished, he made his funny little bow again, put down his bow and walked away, towards the barn. After disappearing inside, he reappeared with a tin of white paint and a brush, ambled over to the cart, and oh so delicately, painted the circles of a target around each embedded arrow, making sure, of course, that each arrow was in the dead centre of each target. He then turned to the assembled audience and beamed a most extraordinary smile of achievement.

The assembled men dare not look at each other or their king, for they were expecting an explosion of fury. But instead, they heard their king laugh. Gentle to begin with but then turning raucous in seconds. The men were confused. Should they join in the laughter? Should they remain silent?

The king set off down the field towards the beaming man. From a distance – a safe distance – the men waited to see what the king did next. To their amazement, he shook the man by the hand, using his other to ruffle his hair. He clasped the man in a hug and walked back to the astonished onlookers with his hand firmly on the farm worker's back.

'This man has demonstrated skills that none of you, none of my countrymen, have ever shown me. Pure joy and honesty.'

The farmhand was rewarded with a small bag of gold, and he was asked to come to the palace the next day.

From that day, the king changed his outlook on life as he now looked for the best in his citizens and their exploits in life. The kingdom remained successful … and, of course, happy.

And I would love to think that the king took the farmhand to the archery competition, complete with tin of paint and a brush.

14

THE RICH MAN

The first time I read this story, it just did not make any sense to me. I thought about it for many days, and then when carrying out a common task (ironing!), it suddenly came to me. Ah, yes, of course!

There had been heavy snow, and now it had begun to clear a little, everywhere was covered in treacherous ice.

A rich man was carefully treading his way across the street. He was dressed in heavy silken robes, had many golden chains hanging around his neck, and over his white stock-inged feet he wore wooden sandals – not the best shoes to be wearing when walking on ice. Sure enough, as he gingerly stepped back onto the pathway, his wooden shoes skidded on the glassy surface, he flew up into the air and crashed onto the freezing ground in a heap. Because of his robes, his chains and his shoes, no matter how he tried, he could not get back on his feet again. Other pedestrians passed by, making their way carefully on the ice. He pleaded for help, holding out his gold-covered fingers, hoping someone would take his hand and help. But no. They all saw a despised, rich man and refused to stop to help.

The nobleman had lain there on the frozen ground for some time when he saw a young Buddhist monk coming towards him. The monk was wearing flimsy saffron robes and was barefooted. The rich man stretched out his hand, asking for help. The young man stopped and smiled at him, and then lay on the ground beside him.

15

CROSSING
THE DESERT

(JATAKA 2)

There was once a young man, born into a family of merchants. It was obvious that he, too, would become a successful merchant. He travelled with five hundred carts and many men, and because of his skills, he and his men made a good living.

One time, they were travelling through a wide and arid desert. It was so hot that the carts would form a circle, put up shading and spend the whole of the day resting, only travelling when the temperatures had dropped in the darkness of the evening. The sand was fine and made journeying hard, especially in the darkness.

On the last part of the journey, the young merchant realised that they would soon be out of this desert, so when their evening meal was over, he ordered everyone to throw all the heavy water jars and crates of food out of the carts to make their onward journey easier. The lower weight would mean that the wheels of the carts would not sink as much in the fine sand. Their journey into the night began.

The pilot, in the front cart, guided the rest of the caravan by the stars and they made good progress. But the evening was warm, the pilot's cart rocked from side to side and soon he was asleep. With no one to guide them, the oxen lost their way, and no one noticed that they had turned around and travelled all the way back, past the previous evening's campsite and onwards. Only when his cart bumped over a rock did the pilot wake up and shout, 'Stop!' The caravan was turned around and made its way back across the desert. When the sun began to rise and the heat became too intense to travel they pulled up to make camp in the same place they had camped the night before, only this time they had no food or water. They made a circle and put up the shading and tried to sleep, but hunger and thirst kept them awake, and the oxen bellowed for water, too.

The young merchant was worried. Without food, water or firewood they would perish, unless he did something about it. He paced up and down and then noticed a patch of desert grass growing in a thick tussock. The grass needed water to grow. He shouted to his men to bring shovels and directed them to begin digging around the grass. The fine sand was difficult to clear away, and they continued to dig without success. One by one, the men gave up in despair, especially when they hit a slab of rock. In the end, there was just one lad left, helping the merchant. 'Surely,' thought the merchant, 'if the grass is so green, there must be water to feed it.' He directed the young lad to climb down into the hole with a hammer and bash the rock. At last, it split from end to end, and, as it did so, the stream it had been damming gushed forth. The men and the beasts could quench their thirsts.

Next day, they carried on to their destination, where they traded successfully and made a great fortune, thankful that their young master the merchant had faith and experience.

Untiring, deep they dug that sandy track
Till, in the trodden way, they water found.
So let the sage, in perseverance strong,
Flag not nor tire, until his heart find Peace.

16

Grandma's Blackie

Some stories just 'hit the spot', and this is one of them for me. I guess it is the reference to family, and in this case a non-standard family – such an important discussion in the world today.

As soon as she saw him, she fell in love. Maybe it was his eyes, his gentleness, his unassuming nature or the promise of such strength – maybe a mixture of them all – but as soon as she saw that beautiful, pure black bull calf, she knew he was special. He came home to live with her, and from the beginning she treated him like her child. She had been alone for so long.

Even though she had little money, she fed him on the best food she could find. He slept on her furniture, and she patted him and stroked his ears until he fell into a snooze, breathing contentedly and feeling safe. She had named him Blackie, as he was velvety black with not a hint of any other colour on him. But because he was always with the woman wherever she went, the village folk called him Grandma's Blackie.

Of course, in time, the calf grew into a huge bull, quite intimidating to a stranger, but he remained gentle and sweetly tame. The local children adored him, and he allowed them to climb on his back and ride him, sometimes swinging on his horns, and he continued to live close to the old woman.

But one day, as he lay in the shade chewing the cud, he began to think about the old woman. 'She is such a kind, old woman, who has raised me almost as if I am her child. I know she does not have much money and must work to support us both, but she is too humble to expect me to work too. I love her just as much and I must help her to escape the suffering of poverty.' So, he decided to look for paid work.

One day, after heavy rain, a travelling caravan of five hundred carts came to the village but had to stop when it came to the swift and swollen river. The bullocks were just not strong enough to pull the carts across. The caravan master even tried hooking up all fifty pairs to one cart but still they were no match for the flowing water.

Mmmm … the caravan master had a problem. He needed to cross to continue his journey, and so he looked round the village to see if he could find more bullocks to help. On spotting the huge black bull, he guessed he had found the answer. He was a good judge where cattle were involved.

He went to the villagers and asked them who owned the bull. 'Oh, he belongs to an old woman, but she is at the market.' They were sure she wouldn't mind if the caravan master used the bull to help. So, he slipped a rope around Grandma's Blackie's neck, clicked his tongue and began to lead the bull to the river. But he instantly came to a halt: the bull was going nowhere. 'I am not moving anywhere until the man promises to pay me for my work.'

The caravan master understood the bull's thoughts and said, 'My strong friend, if you help me move all five hundred carts, I will pay you two gold pieces for each one you move across the river. Not just one piece, but two.' The bull nodded his head and went with the man.

Once down by the river, the caravan master harnessed the huge black bull to the first cart, and he managed to do what a thousand bullocks could not do, swiftly pulling the cart through the raging waters to the other side. He did the same with the remaining carts, without slowing down once.

When all was done, the grateful caravan master made a pouch with five hundred gold coins in it, just one coin for each cart, and hung the pouch around the bull's neck, with his thanks. The bull was an intelligent chap and instantly realised that the caravan master had underpaid him, and so he stood his ground in front of the caravan and would not allow it to pass. The caravan leader tried to drive the bullocks and their carts around him, but the bullocks had seen how strong the black bull was and would not challenge him.

The caravan master realised what an intelligent beast the bull was. He took the pouch back, filled it with the correct amount, and again hung it around the bull's neck. On realising that he had now been paid the correct amount, Grandma's Blackie stood aside, allowing the caravan to progress on its way.

When it had disappeared, the black bull crossed back over the river and made his way back to the house where he lived with the old woman. The children ran with him; they had seen the whole thing. When the old woman saw the pouch swinging from the neck of her 'child', she was surprised, and even more so when she opened it up. The children told her the whole story.

The old woman looked into the exhausted eyes of the bull and said, 'Oh, my son, why did you think you had to work so hard for me? I have no wish to live on your earnings. I can't let you suffer so. No matter how difficult the times are, I will always care and look after you.'

Then the old woman washed the mud from the bull and rubbed soothing oils on his tired muscles. She fed him the best food she could find and looked after him until the end of their happy lives together.

17

THE WOODEN BOWL

I find this story incredibly moving. This version comes from Northern Europe, although there is a similar story from Southeast Asia. But then the story would have to be called The Coffin. Much more hard hitting.

The old man had to wipe away a tear when he arrived at his son's house. His son and his young wife were standing on the veranda with huge smiles on their faces, waiting to welcome their house guest. It was a big day. Father was coming to live with them. For good.

Inside, his room had been prepared on the ground floor, with a comfortable bed and pieces of furniture and bedding from his old home, to make him feel comfortable. The young wife had prepared a lovely meal, and the three of them sat down together to eat and raise a glass to their new venture.

'Welcome father, to our home. We wish you a long and happy life with us. This is now your home, too. Welcome.'

The old man put his hand on top of his son's hand and smiled at his cherished daughter-in-law. 'It is so wonderful to be with family. I am sure I will be happy here, especially if I can be of some help around the farm. There is still some strength left in these old bones.'

They all laughed together. 'You must do what you feel capable of father but also rest when you need to.'

The next morning, the old man put on his work clothes and after breakfast made his way down to the farmyard. He found the hen food and filled the little wooden bowl with it and scattered it for the fowl. He watched as the cockerel proudly pecked the ground around his wife and chickens. 'Oh, to be young again,' he thought.

Each day, he carried out as much work as he could to help his son, and then in the evening he would wash, change his clothes and join them for supper. He noticed with pride how his daughter-in-law's belly was beginning to swell and thought fondly of the time when he would see his grandchild join the family. They noticed how he rubbed the joints in his hands to help with the pain of old age.

Time passed and a new grandson did indeed add to their little family. The old man held the newborn, and reminisced about holding his first born.

'Be careful how you hold him,' said his daughter-in-law. 'Your hands are trembling.'

It was true. The old man had noticed it, too. That dull pain had become a constant worry.

'Don't drop him,' she said, as she took the baby from his arms.

Over time, the changes in the old man's health became more and more noticeable. He found it difficult to walk down to the farmyard, and when he was there he had trouble holding on to the wooden feeding bowl. He would sit on the veranda for most of the day and watch his grandson playing. His son tried to ignore his father's ageing.

By the time the child could walk, the old man had great difficulty in walking, and consequently did little around the farm to help his son. Times became hard. The hired help had to be let go, and the young wife took on the work. The old man tried hard to mind the child.

One night, after a particularly hard day in the fields, the son and his exhausted wife sat down to a simple meal of porridge, prepared by grandfather. He carried each bowl to the table separately, and when at last he filled his own bowl and sat at the table next to his grandson, the old man's hands were so tired he spilled porridge all over the floor.

'How clumsy,' snapped the wife.

The old man was embarrassed and left the table. The son sat and said nothing, as his wife cleaned up the mess.

Each day, the old man's worsening health was more noticeable. He had begun to drool when eating, so the wife set up a place at a small table in the corner, away from the family as they ate.

One evening, the old man knocked his pottery bowl off his little table and it broke as it crashed to the floor. The wife went out to the barn and came back with the wooden bowl used for feeding the hens. She filled it with more soup and placed it in front of the old man.

'Here is one you can't break,' she said. Her husband stared out of the window and didn't say a thing.

The young child by now was older and could speak and play on his own outside the farmhouse. One day his parents found him working hard with a sharp stone, chipping away at two blocks of wood.

'What are you making?' asked his father.

'Oh, I am making a present for you and mama.'

'And what could they be?' asked his father.

'I am making two more chicken feeding bowls that I can give to you when you are old.'

The young man and his wife froze at these words. Each suddenly imagined their future where they too would become elderly.

They turned and looked at each other and went back into the house. They saw father-in-law, frail and alone, sitting in the corner.

The son gathered his father in his arms and carried him to the family table, where his wife had laid him a place, using their best dishes and plates. The child watched as his father fed his grandfather with a spoon and his mama dabbed the drool from the corners of the old man's mouth.

From that day on, they cared for the old man as they hoped their son would care for them when they grew old.

18

THE GOLDEN
MALLARD

(JATAKA 136)

This is similar to 'The Goose that Laid the Golden Eggs'.

There was once a beautiful mallard. His feathers were of the brightest, beaten gold, each one a miniature work of art, and wherever he stood, swam or flew, the sun glittered and sparkled. He was a clever bird, too, because, for some reason, he was aware of his previous life. Near his lake was a village, and at the edge of the village was a ramshackle old house where a woman and her two daughters lived. They were poor, barely making a living, and that made the mallard sad, as in his previous life he had been the woman's husband and the girls were his daughters. His death had hit them hard in so many ways. He therefore decided to visit them.

He landed on the beams in the little house and flapped his golden wings. The woman and her daughters were taken by surprise by this beautiful visitor and asked him why he had visited them. He spoke to them kindly, telling them that he used to be their father and after his sudden death had been reborn as a mallard. He had come to visit them to help them out of their dire straits. He plucked one single feather from his body and dropped it to the ground. One of the girls picked it up and gasped with delight. Not only did it look like gold, it *was* gold. The mallard told them they could sell the feather and live well from the money they would make. He would return from time to time with another feather for them to sell, and they would never know poverty again.

And this is what he did. The woman and the girls sold each feather and soon became prosperous. Their house was rebuilt, they wore beautiful clothes and ate the best of foods. Their life was good.

But the woman became greedy and one day said to the girls, 'How can we trust this mallard and what he says? He is, after all, a wild creature. How can we be sure that one day he won't fly away and never be seen again? Next time he comes, I am going to catch him and pluck out all his feathers. And you will help me.'

The girls were horrified by this suggestion. The mallard had been their father and had been so kind to donate his feathers to them. Why would he suddenly change his mind about helping them? And the task of plucking out all the feathers at once would cause distress and pain to the mallard. No, they would not even think of it.

But the next time the mallard landed on the beam and dropped one of his golden feathers, the mother moved as quick as lightning. She stood on a chair and grabbed the bird with both hands before he could fly away. Clambering down, she held him firmly and told the girls to come to help, but they ran outside in tears.

And she began to pluck the feathers. But as she plucked each tantalising golden feather, it turned white as it fell to the ground. You see, in order for the feathers to remain golden, they had to be given willingly. The faster she plucked, the faster the feathers lost their golden preciousness. The poor bird was now completely bald and in great pain. The woman was angry with the outcome and threw the mallard into a barrel, deciding to feed him and wait for new golden feathers to grow. But as they grew, they returned brown, and grey, and blue, and all the other beautiful colours of a mallard, but not a single golden one was to be seen. One day, when she took the lid off the barrel to throw some food in for him, there was a frantic flapping of wings, and as the woman screamed in terror or anger, the bird escaped and flew out of the house and across the lake, never to be seen by the woman and the girls ever again.

19

THE GLORIOUS STAG

(JATAKA 482)

Deep in a forest, amongst the dappled shade of the tangle of trees, there lived a small herd of deer. At the head of this herd was the most beautiful stag. His fur was golden bright, with patches of marbled colour that shone like gemstones. His eyes were of the deepest blue; wise and piercing. His antlers and hooves shone like polished gold. The stag was a good and caring leader of his herd, and he knew that his appearance was so glorious that, if known about, he would be a magnet for any hunter. And so, he encouraged his family to stay in the shadows, a secret but safe existence.

One day, the herd was down by a fast-flowing river in one of the darkest parts of the forest. Suddenly, they heard the pitiful cries of a human who was being swept along by the swift currents. He would surely drown without help. Without thinking about his own safety, the stag leaped into the water and swam towards the man. Although almost drowning himself, he managed to use his antlers to snag the man's clothing and drag him back to the safety of the riverbank. The man lay there spluttering and spitting water as he recovered, and then he stopped and looked up at his saviour.

The man was amazed at the bravery of the stag and said that he would forever be in his debt, but the deer said there was no need. He did, however, have one favour to ask.

'Anything,' said the grateful man.

The stag asked him never to tell anyone of his existence, as he knew that he would be a sought-after trophy for any hunter. The man agreed, saying that he would not tell a single soul. The man left for his home.

But on his journey home, he noticed a proclamation pinned to a tree at the edge of the forest. It had been posted by the king's men. Apparently, the queen, his wife, had had a dream about the beautiful stag, and she desired the exquisite creature so much that she had persuaded her husband to find it for her. The proclamation announced that if anyone could direct the king to the whereabouts of the magnificent animal, they would be rewarded with wealth and titles.

The proclamation became big news, and the man heard about it every day. He was a good man, but poor, and although he was aware of his promise, he was torn between desire and gratitude. He was eventually overcome with greed and went to the palace to tell the king that he knew where the magnificent stag could be found. The king organised a hunting party and the man led them into the deepest part of the forest. When they arrived, he pointed to where the stag and his herd could be found – and his hand fell off!

The king saw the stag and fitted his finest arrow in his bow. Taking aim, he was about to let loose the lethal bolt, when the stag saw him, and in a human voice, begged the king to stop. The king was amazed at the talking animal and lowered his bow.

'Who told you where to find me?' asked the stag.

The king turned and pointed to the man. The stag approached the man and scorned him, telling him that by breaking his promise, his ungrateful actions were only harming him.

The king asked the stag why he was so angry with the man and the stag told him the whole story. The king turned to the man; he could not believe the deceit.

'You made a solemn promise after your life had been saved and yet you broke it so easily because of your greed for wealth? I curse you, you miserable creature! And as punishment, you will not receive the reward.'

The stag stepped forward and told the king not to be angry with the man, that *his* words of scorn were only to protect him from acting in a similar way again. 'Those lured by the dreams of riches are like innocent moths drawn towards the flames of a fire. They lose all reason and integrity because of their desire.'

The king was impressed by the sympathy of the stag for this man, and decided that he would be given his reward after all. He praised the stag for his wisdom and announced that, from now on, all deer would be safe to walk the kingdom freely.

The stag was grateful and asked if there was anything he could do to recompense the king for his journey into the forest. The king looked at the stag, bowed low and asked if he would accompany him back to the city to speak to the people about his beliefs. The deer accepted and bounded alongside the royal chariot on its way back to the city. Once there, the stag sat on the king's throne and talked to the assembled people, encouraging them to generate compassion for all living beings, to abstain from killing and from stealing, declaring that life should be filled with joy for all.

The king applauded the stag for his wise words and said that from then on, all animals in the kingdom would be respected and protected.

The glorious stag returned to the forest to continue his life in the knowledge that he and his herd, and all other creatures, could live their lives safely, away from the predatory desires of the hunter.

20

EAST AND WEST

This is the first time I have ever 'told' this story. Until now, it has been a jumble of ideas and research notes that I simply could not formulate into a narrative, simply telling audiences the bullet points and asking them if they thought it was interesting enough to compose a story. Most agreed it was. So, here it is at last. The story is simply that: a story. I outline at the end where the ideas come from. I must warn you, it has a description of a cruel form of capital punishment in detail.

The three men found themselves sitting together at the same table in the tavern. They had never met before and as they waited for the owner to bring them their food they attempted to make conversation. Each one was from a different land, and although richly dressed they had the bedraggled look of long-distance travellers, alone in a foreign country and now trying to make sense of the noise and rabble of an overly busy tavern.

They began in faltering Arabic and hand gestures and gradually began to throw in chunks of Greek and Latin. And although at times the noise around them was deafening, they soon began to listen to each other's stories as they drank and ate well into the night. And, as many of the other guests began to retire to their rooms, the place quietened somewhat, and the three men continued their talk and were amazed by the serendipity of their meeting, so far from their homes.

Two of the men asked if they could move closer to the fire, as they were beginning to feel the cold of the night, and the third, although agreeing, laughed as he removed his outer layer of furs.

They had all travelled many miles, all following a quest, all guided by the words in their holy books, the stars and their judgement, and all three sat upright and then leaned inwards as they realised that their missions were the same. Studies, predictions and hopes had led them all to this very same place and, as such, the three decided to travel on the next day in each other's company. They journeyed in search of a new leader, a king or messiah.

The travelling was difficult. The roads were filled with so many people, all making their way to their hometown to register and pay taxes to their despised overlords, the Romans. But these three were strangers in this land, not sure where they were heading. Each had servants to hand, equipment and funds to pay their way, and the determination to continue until they found whatever it was they were looking for.

The palace of the local king seemed a good place to find a king. But as soon as they were in his presence, they knew this was not the man they sought. He was a frightened and angry man. A king in name only. Not a leader, someone who could inspire and change minds, no. They pitied him if the truth were known, a colourful bird in a cage.

They moved on, continually consulting their maps of the heavens, each continually struck by how much his own mission was in tune with the others'.

And then they found it. In a small village, crowded with travellers, filled with Roman soldiers, illuminated by a full moon and its accompanying bright star. A back room, no more than an animal shelter, a humble space, the resting place of a simple family – mother, father and newly delivered child. Peace and tranquillity in a traumatic world and possibly the answer to all their prayers.

All they could do was to sit on the straw of the shelter, look at the tired face of the mother, the anguished face of the father and the serene beauty of this child. Visitors came and went, but the travellers stayed. They said no words; they hardly looked at each other; they still didn't know if this was what they had been looking for.

When at last the three did depart, the young mother held out the baby, wrapped tightly in a cloth, for them to take one last look. Her face was now radiant.

Outside, the three said their goodbyes. None gave any indication what he would do next. They had much to think about. Much to decide.

The travellers from the North and the South both decided that this was indeed a most wonderful experience that promised much for the future, but they needed to consult more with their research and writings. Each decided to continue his search. Malachite, the traveller from the East, although agreeing that this child was not whom he was searching for either, decided to remain, to stay close by. He had a deep-seated feeling that the signs and the testaments were too powerful not to mean something magnificent was happening here. He sent his servants home to report back on the news and found himself lodgings as best he could. He became a constant presence in this family's life.

They trusted him. A kind, wise man, who did not intrude but was there to listen and give advice when asked for. They were in turmoil, too, ordinary folk who realised that their lives would never be the same as others'. They needed someone wise to be close. To interpret dreams. To make sense of the confusion around them. To keep them safe.

After a time, the family journeyed back to their home-town and began 'ordinary' life again. The father settled back into his trade, the mother created a home, and the child grew and prospered. They had become an ordinary, extraordinary family, living a good life amongst good people. The family grew, the parents worked hard, and the child, a boy amongst so many other children in the town, thrived with the love and guidance of family life, and the ever-present Malachite.

The boy was, in almost every way, one of many children playing, studying, working and growing in this vibrant town. He was thoughtful, gentle even, and as he grew older, he began to work alongside his father. It was his time at the Temple that set him apart from the others. He could be found sitting, at first in the shadows, listening to the sermons, discussions and teachings as a youngster, but as he grew, so did his wisdom and his thirst to learn. He moved out of the shadows and began to ask questions and to listen. His knowledge of the scriptures pleased the Temple elders but confused his parents. How could they have such an edu-cated, astute child? Was this what he was meant for?

Malachite was there whenever he could be, for the parents and the child, and guided and soothed them to accept this path. As the child grew into an adolescent, then approached manhood, there was an aura developing that all around could sense.

'Is this the true meaning of his life?' asked the mother.

'Should we encourage this understanding of The Word?' asked the father.

'Is it possible that this child, from a poor family, can achieve so much?' asked the elders and priests from the Temple.

'Oh yes,' said Malachite. 'This is his true path. His destiny. Celebrate it.'

And so, the parents let the young lad spend all the time he could in the Temple. The priests allowed him to ask the difficult questions, answered when they could, but equally, listened to his answers, too. He became a man in all but age.

But Malachite had begun to worry about the customs and traditions of this land that was now his home. He had noticed that it was the way that, when a child approached puberty, maybe fourteen years of age, a spouse would be found. They would be legally promised to wed in the future, a family life would be mapped out. Malachite knew that for anyone to become a great teacher, a spiritual leader, they needed to be free of family, free to be able to travel, to have no other meaning in life but teaching and leading.

One night, as the day had come to an end, Malachite sat with the parents in the courtyard of their house. A fire burnt brightly, and the night sky was dark and full of stars. It was a time for truths and for decisions to be made. Malachite talked to the parents about the future for their son.

'But how can we possibly not agree to his betrothal? It is the way!'

'We are an ordinary family. Our neighbours and family will expect it of us!'

'There is a way,' said Malachite.

He talked about their first born.

A plan was agreed. The young man would accompany Malachite on a journey, a journey east, to the land of Malachite's birth. He would spend time in study, free of family constraints, and Malachite promised that not only would he send regular news, but he would also bring the young man back to his family, when the time was right.

They departed secretly, and although their leaving was sad, the family knew this was necessary for the young man to carry on with his calling.

The journey took many months – there was no reason to hurry, and there was so much to learn and experience as they travelled. Eventually, they did reach the land of Malachite, and a warm welcome was awaiting them both. The young man settled into his new life and home well, even though it was so different from the one he was used to. The people, their clothes and food, their language and customs were enthralling but it was sitting at the feet of the wise elders and religious leaders that captivated the young man.

He found it difficult to begin with. He was used to the teachings of his own scriptures, which were so different from what he was now hearing. An eye for an eye and promises of dreadful judgement were replaced with the notions of treating others how you yourself would want to be treated; looking at one's own faults before judging others and living a respectful and kind life that would lead to a fulfilling future.

And here was a society that lived by those ideas. Where children, the sick and the poor, the elderly and even those cast out, were cared for. Yes, there was still the rich, the religious teachers and political leaders, but it was a fair society, built on truths.

And the young man soaked up this new way of looking at life, saw the power it brought with it, and the fairness of it all. From a student, he gradually became a teacher himself, spending time talking to groups of people large and small, becoming respected by many but always remaining one of the people. And taking time to sit still, alone and contemplate.

But after many years, the young man began to think of his homeland and his family. Not only did he miss them, but he realised there was so much to do there, and it was his calling to return and talk about the new ways.

Malachite was elderly by now but only too happy to return to the land of the young man. This time the journey was more urgent, the desire to reach home took over.

At last they were there.

There were many preachers and teachers travelling from town to town, peddling their brand of rebellion, a dangerous calling in an occupied land. They were driven men. Many were cast out by townsfolk as being possessed and foolish, dangerous even, but some were welcomed, listened to, followed. If this following became too large, too loud, the authorities would become uneasy. The religious leaders would claim blasphemy, Herod would fear that his people would demand more of him, and the Romans hated opposition of any kind. When this displeasure was felt by all three, then it could only mean one thing for anyone overstepping the mark: death.

There was incredible legal machinery in the country to silence any opposition. Religious law was powerful; national law was efficient; and Roman law was ultimate and precise.

And so it was that the young man fell foul of the law and petty jealousies of the various factions. His end was in sight. Malachite had to form a plan quickly if this young teacher were to survive.

The Romans had brought many forms of torture and death penalties to support their rule in occupied lands. These brought fear to the population and were a constant reminder of who was in charge. Crucifixion was one of the most extreme and barbaric of these ways of killing.

It was public and shocking. The criminal carried their own beam of death to the execution place. The nailing to the beam through wrists and ankles made escape impossible. They would be left to hang for days as they fought to keep upright to breathe, the end coming naturally through utter exhaustion, or, if the soldiers could be bribed, a stab, the breaking of legs, or poison would bring about a swift end. But the bodies were often left to decay publicly, a constant reminder to all that this could so easily happen to you.

Malachite worked hurriedly in the background. No one could truly know how he achieved it but somehow he did. He had money, connections and possibly the ear of Herod's wife, the queen, who had become a follower of the young man's teachings.

There was no way to escape the brutality of the initial crucifixion. Later, Malachite persuaded the soldiers guarding the scene that a sponge filled with water to quench the young man's thirst was in fact vinegar. The soldiers would have enjoyed this torment. Malachite had laced the water with a medication, bitter in taste, but swift acting to render the body in such a deep stupor that, to the untrained eye, it would look like death had come quickly. Orders had been given that when death occurred, this body could be taken down for burial. Perhaps this is where the queen had become involved? Sure enough, the body was respectfully taken down, wrapped in shrouds and taken to a tomb prepared in the city graveyard. The entrance was closed with a huge stone. Perhaps unknown to the authorities, there was a rear entrance, and under cover of the night, the unconscious body of the young man was stolen away and carried to safety. After a time of recuperation and secret goodbyes, Malachite steered the young man to permanent safety, back to the country in the East.

The young man lived his life there, teaching and guiding others, and garnered such respect that, when in old age he finally died, he was placed in a tomb that became a place of pilgrimage. A life well lived.

There is much written discussing the missing eighteen years in the life of Jesus, from twelve to twenty-nine years of age. A period between boyhood and the beginnings of his ministry that is not mentioned anywhere in the Bible.

Equally, there is much discussion about whether Jesus died on the cross. Islam, for instance, regards Jesus as a major saint, and believes strongly that he did not die on the cross, but that God raised him to him, someone else having taken his place at the execution.

There have been several accounts of Jesus spending some time in India, usually at the end of his life. For the purpose of my story, I have included the missing years and end-of-life accounts:

Nicolas Notovich, Life of Saint Issa, Best of the Sons of Men, *1887. Notovich claimed to have been shown a document in a Buddhist monastery in the Himalayas which told of Jesus spending time in the area. It caused controversy at the time and many disproved his claims. It is suggested that he confessed to having fabricated the whole story.*

Swami Abhedananda, 1922 from New York, travelled to the monastery and claimed to have seen the scroll Notovich had described. After his death, one of his disciples travelled to the monastery, where he was told that the scroll had disappeared.

Nicholas Roerich, 1925, travelled through Ladak, in India, and spoke to communities in the area who told him ancient stories that were remarkably similar to accounts in Notovich's book.

Roza Bal Shrine: In 1899, Mirza Ghulam Ahmad wrote a book called Masih Hindustan-mein *(Jesus in India). It declares that a tomb found in the town is the resting place of Jesus, who had travelled to the valley looking for one of the lost tribes of Judaism. It has been discredited but is still a place of pilgrimage for Christians, Muslims and Buddhists.*

The majority of modern Christian writers and theologians all discredit the above claims. I include this story with respect.

21

THE NOISE
THE HARE HEARD

(JATAKA 322)

Here is a wonderful story that you might recognise in another form, as a Brothers Grimm folk tale. Other versions are told in Scandinavia, too.

The hare stretched out, half asleep, under the sapling where he had made his home. The sapling grew in a plantation of vilva trees, and the dappled shade of their leaves made it a cool place to spend the afternoon. But this afternoon, the hare was troubled by something, and soon his thoughts turned to dark questions, like, what would happen to him if the earth came to a sudden end? Just as he thought this, a heavy ripe fruit from one of the trees fell from its branch and thudded on a large leaf near to the hare. He sat up in terror. The world was coming to an end, he had just heard it breaking up! And with that, he took flight, running through the jungle at breakneck speed, not looking over his shoulder.

A fellow hare saw him running, terrified, and asked him what the problem was. 'Oh please, don't ask me, it is too terrible,' said the hare, but the second hare pressed him for an answer. 'The world is coming to an end! I just heard a piece break off, and I am running to safety.' With that, he set off running again, this time with the second hare, running just as fast. As they scurried through the jungle, more hares asked them what the problem was and, hearing the answer, joined in the flight. Soon there were other animals stopping and questioning them; elephants, tigers, monkeys, parrots, zebras, mice, snakes; and when each heard of the problem, they joined in the flight, all heading from the west to the east, towards the great sea. At last, the King of the Lions saw the huge herd of creatures hurtling towards their death, a dusty, frantic drive, running towards the cliffs and their fate. He knew he must do something to stop them. Taking three huge leaps and bounds, he landed in front of the stampede and growled three enormous growls. The animals skidded to a sudden halt, now cowering in terror at the lion in their path.

'Why are you all running? What has caused you all so much terror?' he demanded.

'The earth is collapsing!' they all shouted.

'But who saw the earth collapsing?' he asked.

'The elephants know,' said some of the animals. But the elephants said they didn't know but that the tigers know. The tigers shook their heads and said the monkeys know. The monkeys said they didn't, but the parrots know, and then the zebras, and then the mice, and then the snakes, and then the hares, and then the hares pointed to one particular hare. 'He knows,' they said.

'Well?' asked the lion.

'Oh, I can't tell you!' howled the hare.

'Then show me,' ordered the lion, and he instructed the hare to jump on his shoulders. The lion told the other animals to stay exactly where they were until he returned, and the lion and hare leaped over the animals' heads and headed back to the west where the hare had first come from. But as they got nearer to the plantation, the hare began to whimper loudly, so loudly in fact, that the lion pulled up and the hare climbed down. Between his terrified howls, he pointed to the area where he had heard the earth breaking, and the lion bounded through the trees and into the vilva plantation. He stood for a while, catching his breath, taking pleasure from the shady coolness and the stillness, when 'thump!', there was a huge thud as another ripe fruit crashed onto a large leaf as it fell from the tree. He stood a little while longer and then again it happened, and again. It wasn't the earth breaking up, it was the sound of dropping ripe fruit, and the sleepy hare had imagined the worst.

He ran back to the hare and got him to climb onto his back once more, and the two of them ran at the speed of a speedy lion until they were again in front of the herd of animals. Once the hare had dismounted, the lion told them all that he had discovered, much to the embarrassment of the hare. They all raised their eyebrows, made their own version of a loud, 'tut', and turned and made their way home, vowing next time to check before they jumped to conclusions.

22

THIEF!

A strange short story.

A Buddhist monk had just completed a period of fasting as part of his devotions. He had only sipped water during the several weeks of abstinence, and although he felt refreshed and renewed from his experience, he was looking forward to getting back to the monastery and eating again.

On his short journey back, many of the townspeople stopped the monk to congratulate him on his achievement, and, trying not to show any pride, he thanked them kindly. But his stomach churned at the thought of food and he hurried on.

Then he met a very devout young couple, who held his hands humbly and showered him with praise.

'Please,' they asked, 'please will you join us in our humble abode and break your fast with us?'

The monk was taken aback by this request. Their praise and their generous offer touched him. And it would mean that he would eat sooner than going home and having to prepare his own food.

As they bowed and walked backwards, they led him into their house. There was a low table set with bowls of wonderfully aromatic food and they invited the monk to sit on the cushions near the table. The monk sat down and reached to sample the food.

'Oh please,' said the woman. 'I have not laid out everything yet, please wait for the hot food.'

The monk reined in his hand as the couple scuttled into the kitchen, where there were noises of stirring and scooping of spoons in pans. The monk sat in front of the food, breathing in all the aromas and casting his gaze across all the cold foodstuffs.

At last, the couple brought in bowls with steaming food in them and placed them in front of their guest. He held his tummy to quell the rumbling noises and again reached forward to help himself.

'Oh no, please,' said the young woman again. 'I must wash your hands for you.' And the two of them left the room once more and the monk could hear them heating water. He began rocking backwards and forwards as hunger began to overtake him and his whole body seemed to be breathing in this feast before him.

The couple appeared with a bowl of warm water and they both began to reverently wash his hands and dry them. He smiled all the time, on the outside, but so wished he could break his fast soon.

They stood up when they had finished, and the monk's eyes lit up and he nodded his head for permission to start.

'Oh, we need bowls and spoons.'

Again, they hurried out of the room into their kitchen, where they busily collected their best bowls and spoons. But, as she piled the bowls into her husband's arms, they suddenly heard the monk shout, 'Stop, stop thief!'

The woman shrieked and the man dropped the bowls as they looked at each other and ran into their main room to protect their guest. To their amazement they were met with the sight of the monk, alone in the room but holding his right wrist with his left hand and shouting at it, 'Stop thief!'

The wait had become just too much for the hungry guest and he had stolen only a mouthful. Horrified that he may have offended his benefactors by starting before they said he could, he had to reprimand his right hand for stealing.

23

THE SELFLESS HARE

(JATAKA 316)

This is probably one of the most well-known stories from the Jataka tales and is both delightful and horrifying. Delightful in the explanation as to why people living around the Indian sub-continent see a hare when they look at the moon, rather than the face of a man. Of course, they view the moon from a different angle so see a different pattern of craters. And horrifying from the casual mention of self-immolation as part of a sweet story. Again, this would have been viewed from a different angle from those of us in the West. In the time the story was first told, suicide by burning was not unknown, especially when a wife was cremating her husband. I respectfully tell my version here.

In a beautiful forest, filled with exotic plants, ferns and flowers, there lived a wise hare. He was a handsome fellow and loved living in this idyllic home. There were always clearings filled with sunshine and the buzzing of insects, and then there were the secret, shade-filled hidden places, cool enough to sleep in at the height of summer. Vines and fruit trees grew everywhere and a cool, burbling stream snaked its way to who knows where. And there was so much sweet, flavoured grass to eat, the favourite food of the hare.

There were paths that cut through the forest, too, and occasionally respected monks in their flowing saffron robes passed through the forest on their way to and from the monasteries in the mountains. These monks survived on alms, gifts of food – and it was considered a holy duty to give alms whenever one could.

The hare had three close friends, who looked upon him as their leader: a monkey, a jackal and an otter, and they trusted him to keep them on the straight and narrow, especially when it came to remembering moral laws. He would remind them as any holy days approached that even though they were animals, if anyone should ask them for food, they should freely and generously give of whatever they had collected to eat for themselves.

Indra, lord of all the gods, was watching the forest from his palace in the heavens one holy day and overheard the hare talking to his friends so earnestly. He decided to test their virtue.

That special day, the four friends had separated and made their way to their favourite places in the forest to look for food. The otter was down by a pool created by the stream, and he had laid out on its bank seven beautiful red-and-black, striped fish. The jackal had caught a lizard and had found a discarded jug with some curdled milk in it. The monkey had climbed high into the trees and filled his arms with sweet and juicy mangoes.

Indra, who had taken the form of a priest, a Brahman, approached the otter and said, 'My good friend, I am so hungry. I need food before I can carry out my priestly duties. Can you help me please?' The otter remembered the words of the hare and offered the Brahman the seven fish he had caught for his own meal.

The Brahman gave thanks and then moved on and found the jackal. 'My good friend, I am so hungry. I need food before I can carry out my priestly duties. Can you help me please?' The jackal, remembering his friend the hare, gave the lizard and the curdled milk that he had planned for his own meal that evening.

The Brahman again gave thanks and moved on to find the monkey, who was just climbing down the tree. 'My good friend, I am so hungry. I need food before I can carry out my priestly duties. Can you help me please?' The monkey looked at the sweet fruits cradled in his arms and thought of the words of the hare. He gave the Brahman the mangoes that he had been so looking forward to feasting on that night.

The Brahman gave thanks and moved further down the path to find the hare, who was sitting in a sunlit clearing. 'My good friend, I am so hungry. I need food before I can carry out my priestly duties. Can you help me please?'

The hare looked around. He had no food other than all the lush, sweet grass growing around him in the forest, not food for a human. So, the hare asked the Brahman to build and light

a fire in the clearing. When the fire was burning good and strong, the hare said, 'I have nothing to give you to eat except myself.' And in a second, the hare threw himself into the fire.

Indra was amazed and deeply moved by the actions of the hare. Quickly, he caused the fire to burn coldly so that the hare was not harmed by the flames, and the hare hopped out. The Brahman then respectfully revealed his identity to the selfless hare. 'Dear Hare, your virtue will be recognised throughout time.' The Brahman reached into the sky and painted the wise hare's likeness on the beautiful pale moon, for all to see down the ages.

24

The King of the Water Buffalo

The King of the Water Buffalo was a splendid chap. Although he was as strong as, well, an ox, he was also a creature of great character. He was unassuming, kind and gentle, full of compassion and empathy, and possessed the highest of morals. He was greatly liked and respected by all the other buffalo, who would cluster around him to be near.

One day, the king and his herd made their way to a riverbank close by. The water flowed slowly, deep and crystal clear. The grasses on the riverbank grew thickly and the waterweed was sweet to munch. The bank of the river sloped gently into the water, making plenty of room for the buffalo to wander around, bathe, wallow and sleep. It was so pleasant a place, they decided to make their home there for a time.

Not far from the river was a plantation of trees growing in a clump, and there a macaque monkey lived with his family in the branches. The next time the monkey took his family down to the river to drink, he was shocked to see the buffalo herd living there. He sat on a washed-up tree trunk and watched the King of the Water Buffalo, and took notice of the extraordinary behaviour of this mountain of an animal. He was so serene and had a huge following. Seeing all this made the monkey envious, and suddenly he raised himself up on the log and began shouting all kinds of abuse at the buffalo. When the Buffalo King took no notice, the monkey, now enraged, jumped onto the riverbank, picked up pebbles and began hurling them. 'Get away from here!' he shouted. 'This is my territory! You take your herd and leave my place at once.'

The king looked up, still munching his sweet grass, and then put his head down again and grabbed more greenery. Not only did he not retaliate but he also kept calm, protecting his heart from anger, silently receiving all that was hurled at him.

A little time later, another part of the herd returned from a neighbouring pasture to join their tribe, and began munching and drinking. The monkey was incandescent with rage. He picked up more rocks and threw them, and more insults, at the new group of buffalo. But having observed the reaction of their king to the previous onslaught, they too ignored the monkey with tolerance and acceptance, and, having their fill of sweet water, calmly and quietly wandered back to the pasture.

Not far away was a young buffalo who had strayed from the herd. He witnessed both attacks by the monkey, and being young and full of bluster, he wanted to teach the monkey a lesson in respect. But he realised quickly that his elders were teaching him an important lesson through their experience of life, and he, too, ignored the naughty monkey and continued munching the greenery.

When the heat of the sun became so strong that the buffalo needed shade to sleep in, they wandered across to another grove of trees. In the middle of this grove was a large and mighty tree, which just happened to be a tree god. As the Buffalo King lay down to snooze in the shade, the tree said, 'I have just seen what happened between you and that rascal of a monkey and yet you did not retaliate. You are a mountain of a creature and would have had no problem in dealing with him. Yet you chose to ignore him. May I ask you why?'

The Buffalo King was still chewing the cud, and between chews he said, 'Everything in this world is at the mercy of cause and effect, everything we do has consequences. That monkey shouted abuse and threw stones at me, and no doubt this is the way he treats all other animals he meets. If he carries on behaving in this way, one day there will be consequences of his bad actions … he will meet his match. How could I possibly hurt someone who is so ignorant of life? And if I had acted against him, well, with my huge weight and strength, I would no doubt have taken his life, which would have resulted in me being subject to retribution in my future. Where is the good in any of that? Staying calm and maintaining self-control is really the best protection for one's own life, too.'

And with that, the King of the Water Buffalo swallowed the cud, rolled over and slept soundly.

25

THE SEVEN PRINCES

(JATAKA 193)

*When I first read the translation of this Jataka tale, I was rather
taken aback. To modern ears it is so politically incorrect and
difficult to read, but I have included it. It is a narrative of the
times, over two thousand years ago. One of the Buddha's disciples fell in love with a woman he saw whilst out collecting alms.
When he returned to life in the monastery, he became depressed
and ill and could not concentrate on meditation because of the
image of the woman he carried in his mind. The Buddha told
him this story to remind him that women can be a burden to
an aesthetic.*

In a previous life, the Buddha was once the crown prince of
a beautiful land. He and his six brothers loved their father
dearly and served him as well as they could, but for some
unknown reason the father suspected his sons of wanting to
kill him and take the throne. His paranoia finally got the
better of him and one day he banished all seven sons and
their wives from the kingdom. Not one of them could return
to the country until his father had died.

Of course, they were all deeply saddened and confused, but they could not argue with their father, and so all seven couples packed up some belongings and travelled far away until they reached a forest in another country. The forest offered them no food or drink and soon they became quite frantic with hunger and thirst.

When they could bear it no longer, they took the desperate action of killing the youngest wife, cutting her into thirteen pieces, one for each remaining person, and eating her. The crown prince and his wife shared one piece between them and saved the other piece in a secret place. They did this for five more days, until finally the wife of the crown prince was the only woman left alive. On the seventh day, it was time to kill and eat her, but the crown prince gave his brothers the saved portions and they ate these instead.

That night, he and his wife made a daring escape under cover of the darkness. They hurried through the forest, scrambling over rocks and pushing their way through thick shrubbery. When his wife became tired, he carried her on his shoulders. When she became thirsty, he took his sword and sliced his right knee so she could drink his blood. At last, they reached the safety of the shores of the River Ganges, and there they drank the water, ate the fruit and made themselves a simple hut to live in.

One day, they heard moaning coming from the middle of the river and there was a little boat, floating rudderless, with a strange man on board. The crown prince was able to wade out into the water and bring the boat to land, but when they investigated it, there was a man, a convicted criminal, who had been punished by having his hands, feet, nose and ears cut off, and set adrift in the boat. They gently carried him back to their hut, where they looked after him, bathing and dressing his wounds and feeding him sweet fruit.

The man began to heal well and whilst the crown prince was out each day in the forest collecting fruit, his wife and the criminal fell in love. She decided in time that the only answer was to kill her husband, and one day she followed him as he collected fruit. Spotting her chance, she managed to jump out on him and push him over a cliff to his death.

Fortunately for the crown prince, and unbeknown to his cruel wife, he crashed into a large fig tree that broke his fall. Although he survived, he could not climb down from the tall tree and so he lived in the branches, living on figs. One day, an iguana came climbing in the tree and they struck up a conversation. The crown prince told him his sorrowful story, and the iguana was so moved he took him on his back and carried him down the tree and out of the forest.

The crown prince found refuge for a time in a little village, until the day came when he heard that his father, the king of the neighbouring country, had died. It was time for him to return and claim the crown.

As king, he ruled wisely, and his people loved him. Every day he shared his fortune with the poor by placing food, clothes and money in specially constructed assembly halls.

His ex-wife carried her lover out of the forest on her shoulders, and they managed to earn enough to eat by begging near the temples. The other beggars told her that she should put her husband in a basket and carry him to the capital city, where the king's mercy was well known. They went, and sure enough they lived well on the king's generous alms.

The king was parading through the city, riding on one of his magnificently adorned elephants, when he saw his ex-wife, though she did not recognise him. He called her over to him. She bowed low, but when she heard his voice, she looked up in terror. The king spoke loudly to his people and explained who she was and what evil deeds she had done, and with the crowds encouraging him, he sentenced her to death. But he chose to spare her life. Instead, he had the basket containing her lover tied tightly to her head so that she would never be able to remove it, and banished her from his kingdom.

26

THE TIGER'S WHISKER

This is a story I have heard several times, and many traditions claim 'ownership' of it. I love telling this story.

When anyone saw them together, they realised that they were the perfect couple. From different villages and humble backgrounds, they soon settled to making a life together. Their little house completed, they cultivated the plot of land around them. This done, they began to find ways to earn money. He made furniture and she decorated the pieces with the most beautiful of colours and patterns. And whatever they were doing, they were always talking and laughing, a good sign of a strong marriage.

But then came the stories of troubles near the coast and the capital city. Troubles that had no bearing on their safe and tranquil lives, except when one day, the lorries came rolling into the village. Men were needed to fight in the battles. The men were rounded up and loaded on the backs of these rickety trucks. The last she saw of him was his distraught face looking back at her as the lorry sped from the village, leaving the taste of fear in the diesel fumes.

The stories from the front were terrifying and seemed to make no sense to those left behind in the village. Details were sketchy and few and far between but everyone knew there were casualties from the heavy fighting. Then at last, word came that peace had been agreed. As quickly as the troubles had started, they ceased. The lorries came back to the village and those who had survived climbed down from them to try to restart their lives. She stood watching and waiting, and then she saw him. He was thin and ragged, and she ran and flung her arms around his neck. He was different. He felt tense, rigid. She guided him towards their house and made him food. He slept, there on the floor where he had sat to eat. He had not spoken, he had not fully looked at her, but she had noticed his eyes, dead and lacking any expression.

Give him time, she thought, give him time.

But time did not seem to help. He sat around, listless and without purpose. He refused to talk to her about anything but the simplest of things. He drank and smoked and never came to bed. He was angry, a dark cloud threatening thunder, and then one day it came.

'Will you stop talking woman!' he had shouted, and had raised the back of his hand to her. She had cowered and he had fled outside.

She had no idea how to help or what to do. She could not talk to her friends about this – it would seem disloyal – and her family lived in the next village, a day's trek away. In the end she decided to go to see the wise man. He seemed to have the answer to all problems.

She sat and he stood whilst he listened to her story.

'Can you help me ... us?' she asked.

'Of course I can. There is a solution to every challenge,' he said, kindly.

He went to the back of his house and began to gather ingredients from his shelves.

'Ah, but I have one problem. There is one ingredient I don't have. You will have to provide that.'

'Anything,' she said. 'I can get you anything!'

'Mmmm … the one ingredient I need from you, is the whisker from a tiger, a living tiger.'

There was a long silence, as the enormity of this request sunk in.

'But, but how could I manage that? That is impossible!'

'But it is needed to bring about the solution. There again, if you don't think it is possible, then I am afraid there is noth …'

'No, I'll do it!'

'Good. When you have it, bring it to me here and we will be near to you both finding peace of mind.'

'That's all I wish for,' she said.

She went away, and that evening, whilst her troubled man drank himself to sleep, she sat in the coolness of the evening breeze and made her plan. From a child she had been shown how to avoid the dangerous creatures of the forest and now she was being asked to put herself in danger on purpose. But her marriage was important to her, and she had to try everything to help her husband.

So, next day, she wandered deep into the forest, so deep that the paths were no longer visible, and she had to fight her way through the long grasses and the bushes. At last, she came to a small clearing. The sun shone in through a gap in the forest canopy and the grass grew thick and lush, and there, in the dappled shade, she found the telltale sign of the resting place of a large animal. The grass was trampled and formed into the unmistakable shape of some sleeping creature. She looked round and saw a large tree at the edge of the clearing, a tree with many low branches. She made her way over to the tree and climbed easily into the higher branches, and there she settled to wait and watch. She had not been there too long when she heard crashing in the surrounding scrub. She ceased breathing and watched. Then he appeared. The hugest tiger she had ever seen. She stopped herself from gasping and controlled the shivering of her hands as she held onto the branch she was perched on. She watched as he came into the clearing, sniffed the air, circled in the grass and collapsed in the patch of beaten-down greenery she had spotted. He groomed himself for a time, occasionally stopping and smelling the air as if he could sense something different, but then, satisfied that all was well, he lay down his head and fell into a sleep.

Inside, she wanted to scream. She was truly terrified, but this is what she had come to find. She sat there in silence in the afternoon heat, trying not to fall asleep, and waited to see what happened. At last, the beast awoke, stretched and yawned like a young kitten, sniffed the air once again, got to his feet and sauntered off into the undergrowth. She gave him time to disappear into the forest and then she groaned, tears streaming down her face. This experience was terrifying enough, but how on earth was she going to get close enough to him to pull out a whisker? She climbed down the tree and made her way home. That night, she was the quiet one, as she sat and thought about her next steps.

The next day, she retraced her path and found the clearing again, climbed the tree and waited in the branches. Sure enough, he came back to the resting place at about the same time, and after much sniffing of the air, curled up to take his afternoon nap. Her heart thumped inside her chest, but she knew she must take her next step. Whilst he slept, she gently hummed a tune, keeping an eye on the sleeping animal. Yes, he twitched a little, even opened his eyes occasionally, but he seemed content enough to carry on sleeping. When he began to wake up naturally, she ceased her humming and off he ambled, unconcerned.

And so it continued like this for several weeks, except, as time went on, the young woman hummed a little louder. Again, the tiger stirred a little but never seemed troubled. And then the young woman began to slowly change the humming to gentle singing. Songs that she had learned as a youngster in her village. The tiger did react a little more to this, standing and sniffing the air, but he soon settled down again for his nap.

Over the weeks, the singing turned to storytelling, and as the woman became more confident she didn't climb quite as high into the tree. After more weeks, she sat on the ground. Her stories became more animated.

And then, she began to move closer to the sleeping tiger each day, judging when she should remove herself to behind the tree before he woke up.

At last, her stories began to shift to her just talking to the tiger and sitting close to him. She told him of her family village and of the village she now lived in with her husband. She told him of her husband, of the fine home they had built together and all the crafts they made to sell. And each day, she came closer and closer until at last she was right next to him, able to see his fur, the stripes, the fleas, and his chest, silently heaving up and down as he slept contentedly.

And then, one day, when she began telling him of how her husband had been taken away, she laid her hand on his side and felt his warmth and his strength. She gently moved her hand in a caress, and each day she moved that caress to his head, his ears … his face, telling him about how her husband had come back from the fighting and how he had changed, how he was troubled, uncommunicative and angry. And then one day, she told the sleeping tiger how she had come for his help. How he would never know just how much he had helped. The caress was soft and gentle on his nose. And then, without even breathing, she allowed her fingers to settle on the tiger's whiskers, where she fondled them and rubbed them, and then, oh so carefully, she selected one whisker and plucked it from the tiger's face. She returned to her tree before the tiger woke, and in the shadow and safety of its trunk, she broke down and wept silently. When at last the tiger woke, yawned and stretched, and then rose to his feet to return to his kingdom, she peeped out from behind the tree and gently whispered, 'Thank you my friend … and goodbye.'

And back to the village and the safety of her home she went. She carried her treasured prize carefully and placed it in the drawer of one of her husband's pieces of furniture and for the first time in many, many months, she slept soundly.

Next morning, she was up early. She made food and coffee for her husband and, as he ate, she kissed him on his head, and he looked at her and smiled. Over recent months she had been as quiet as he had in the evenings. He had feared that his raised hand had pushed her too far. He had noticed that she spent much time away from their home and him.

And off she went, to the other side of the village and entered the wise man's home. He was surprised but pleased to see her.

'Have you managed to procure what I asked of you?'

And she proudly opened her hand and there was the beautiful silver whisker. He sat down opposite her, and she told him the whole story. He listened carefully, nodding wisely at her bravery and patience.

At last, he stood up, and she watched him in the light of the central fire as he gathered all his ingredients together on a low table.

'And now, the hard-earned, treasured tiger's whisker.'

She held out her hand and he carefully took the whisker between thumb and forefinger. He held it up to look at it carefully in the light from the fire. She watched him as he held it high in front of them both, and then he dropped it into the flames.

There was a moment's silence before she screamed and scrambled towards the flames.

'What have you done? *What have you done?* she yelled at him.

He quietly sat opposite her, and through the light of the flames he held her stare with his gentle eyes.

'No, what have *you* done?' he asked.

She sat upright, puzzled and tear stained.

'You have shown your absolute devotion to your husband and your marriage by having risked your very life to calm a dangerous creature so that you could pluck a whisker from his muzzle. To save your marriage, save your husband. Think about it. If you can do that, then with the same patience and love, you can surely calm the ferocious beast inside your husband and save him and your life together. Sit with him quietly, hum and sing to him, tell him stories of your village, tell him about the wonderful man you married, how you had planned the perfect life together, how dreadful things happened to him, and you, during the war and how he came home again, and how dearly you want him back again.'

She slowly stood and nodded. She turned and made her way home, gently humming to herself.

27

THE MUSTARD SEED

Death is a subject we generally don't think about much unless it comes to someone we know. However, it is certain we will die, and the time and manner of our death are uncertain. Yet we tend to live our lives as if we are sure we will live to be old and die peacefully in our sleep. We don't consider how fragile our life-force is. … Life or death is only a breath away.

One day, the Buddha was approached by a grief-stricken woman. Her clothes were torn, her face was smeared with tears and her hair a tangle of worry. She was carrying the body of her baby boy in her arms.

'Please master, I plead with you to work a miracle and bring my son back to life!'

She told him that she had waited many years to have a child. The child had died at a young age, and she was inconsolable.

The Buddha smiled at her with compassion. He truly felt her grief and thought deeply for a while how best he could help her. He then told her to go into the village and knock on every door, asking for one grain of mustard from any household where no one had died. He would then see what he could do to help her. The woman smiled at him, and still carrying her dead child, turned and ran off into the village.

She spent all day knocking on doors, asking if anyone had died there and then telling her story to explain why she asked. But she couldn't find any household that had not experienced the death of a family member. By the end of the day, she was exhausted, and had no mustard seeds for all her asking. She sat down in the cool breeze and thought of the Buddha's request and what lesson it might teach her.

'Is it not the nature of all living things that we are born and must surely die?'

It is a difficult fact of life, one that is hard to learn, but it helped her greatly to accept the sad death of her child.

28

THE GOBLINS AND THE MERCHANTS

(Jataka 1)

There was once a successful merchant who travelled backwards and forwards across the known world, with his caravan of ox carts, trading spices, fabrics and carpets. So successful was he that his caravan of carts was large, and he and his workmen made a good living.

He was just about to make a long journey, which included travelling across a wide and arid desert, when he found out that another caravan, led by a young and inexperienced merchant, was about to make the same trek at the very same time. Such journeys had to be planned well in advance, to make sure that the trail was safe, could provide enough food and water for the men, plus firewood for the camps and grassland for the oxen, for the duration. The thought of another, poorly planned caravan journeying the same route worried the experienced merchant, and so he visited the young merchant to hopefully arrange some mutually beneficial plan.

After discussing the situation, it was decided that they should leave at different times, the young merchant electing to set off first.

Unbeknown to either merchant, there was a troupe of goblins who lived in the centre of this desert. There was nothing more delightful to them than the flesh of humans to eat for their supper, and so when they discovered there was a caravan approaching, plans were made to slaughter all the humans. The Goblin King devised a cunning plan to persuade the travellers to discard their drinking water, leaving them thirsty and weak, easy pickings for the goblin hordes.

The Goblin King used his magic powers to create a wonderful carriage that was covered in drapes, which were then soaked in water. His men wore lotus flowers and lush leaves all over their bodies.

The disguised goblins stopped their carriage to talk to the young merchant in his lead cart. The men were looking tired and dusty from their travels.

'Ah, my friends,' said the Goblin King, pushing a lotus flower away from his face. 'You have travelled the worst part of the journey, the rest is easy. In fact, why don't you lessen your load? Ahead there is heavy rain and plenty of lakes full of clear water. Get rid of your heavy water jars, they are just slowing you down, after all. There is plenty of water awaiting you.'

The young merchant had no reason to doubt this advice – after all, look how wet and damp his men and their carts looked. And so, he ordered his men to throw the water jars out of the ox carts, most smashing into pieces as they hit the hard sand.

But, of course, they found no water for the rest of the day and as they traversed through the hottest part of the desert, the merchant and his men became exhausted. They had no water to cook their rice and vegetables, and had to sleep that night thirsty and hungry. The goblin hordes approached in the darkness, slaughtered the men and even the oxen, and devoured every inch of flesh. Bare, white, sucked-clean bones littered the ground where they had slept.

About two months later, the experienced merchant began to journey, too, with his five hundred carts. The goblins could not believe their luck and approached this caravan with the same plan. The men believed the lie and wanted to get rid of the heavy jars of water, but the merchant recognised that this was untrue. He turned to his men and said, 'If there was rain ahead, we would have seen the storm clouds on the horizon, heard the thunder and lightning and felt the winds.' And so, they carried on with their journey as planned. At last, they came to the savaged campsite of the other caravan. They encircled the camp with the five hundred ox carts, and that night half the men had swords in their hands to defend themselves whilst the other half buried the bones in the sand. The furious goblins watched on.

Next morning, much of the merchandise was taken from the carts of the first caravan and loaded into the five hundred ox carts. Their onward journey was a safe one, they traded well and afterwards gave thanks to the deceased traders. They had made a good profit, and all thanks to the experience of their merchant leader.

29

Three Friends

(Jataka 206)

This lovely story reminds me so much of 'The Lion and the Mouse', one of Aesop's Fables.

Once upon a time, a large antelope lived happily in a thicket by the side of a lake. An owl lived high in the branches of the trees and a turtle made his home in the waters of the lake. The three of them were firm friends, often passing the time of day with each other in conversation. Life was good.

But one day, a young hunter came into the area and he spied the footprint of an antelope in the mud. He was experienced and could tell from the imprint that it had been made by a large and fine antelope, one that he wanted to catch and kill. So, as night began to darken, he set a trap made of leather. It was strong leather formed into loops, almost like a metal chain. The hunter went home, planning to return the next morning.

During the night, before he settled down to sleep, the antelope made his way down to the lake for his last drink. As he trod in the lakeside mud, there was a sharp snapping sound, and the trap grabbed his leg in a painful and tight loop. No matter how hard he tried he could not free himself, and he howled in terror and anguish. His friends, the owl and the turtle, heard his cries and rushed to his aid, but again, no matter how hard they twisted or pulled, they could not free the antelope from the grip of the trap.

'What are we going to do?' asked the turtle.

'Well,' said the owl, 'you have such a sharp and strong mouth. You could try biting your way through the straps and I will fly to the home of the hunter and try to delay his return.'

And so, this is what they did. The little turtle chewed and bit as best he could at the strong leather, and the owl quickly flew through the darkness, and, spotting the hunter, followed him to his home.

Next morning, at sunrise, the hunter packed his weapons and smiled at the thought of returning to his trap to find the antelope. He opened his front door and was just stepping over the threshold when the owl bravely flew down at him, fluttering in his face. The hunter was shocked and thought this was a bad omen. He decided to go back into his house to leave it a while before he set off again. He lay down on his bed and slept.

Meanwhile, the little turtle was still biting as best he could through the leather thongs, but it was such hard work for a little fellow. He didn't know when the hunter would return but he did guess that the owl would be working just as hard as he was to save their friend, the antelope.

The owl knew that he had truly spooked the young hunter and he decided that if the hunter were to set off again, he would probably not use the same door. So, cleverly, he flew round to the back door. The hunter, stirring from his snooze, got up and decided once more to go to check his trap – but he would not go out of his front door again, that was bad luck. So, he opened his back door. Again, just as he stepped over the threshold, the owl delivered a glancing blow to the huntsman's face, and the terrified young man turned and slammed the door shut. The omens were against him today, he thought, and decided he would leave it until the next morning to check the trap.

The owl waited a little while until darkness came. He was sure the hunter would not venture out in the dark, and he flew back to the lake. The little turtle was still working away at the leather. He was exhausted and his mouth was bleeding, but he was determined to do everything he could to save his friend. He worked through the night and as the sun was rising, he had just one last piece to bite through. But it was too late, the unmistakable sounds of the hunter approaching could be heard. The antelope said, 'Let me have one last try.' The turtle stepped back, and the antelope kicked with all his might and at last the weakened leather thongs snapped and the antelope was free. 'Escape, quickly!' shouted the turtle. The antelope bounded into the shadows of the undergrowth and the owl flew high into the trees, but the poor, exhausted turtle was too slow, and the hunter caught him. He was furious that he had not caught the antelope, but at least he had a turtle. He placed the turtle in a cloth bag, made his way home, and hung the bag on a hook near his door.

The antelope and the owl had followed. The antelope sprang into action: he had to save his turtle friend now. Swiftly, he sped through the undergrowth and magically appeared in the middle of a nearby clearing, in full view of the hunter. The hunter grabbed his bow and ran nearer the antelope, but the antelope dashed off into the shadows, appearing in full sight again in the next clearing. He lured the hunter further and further into the depths of the forest until at last the hunter was totally lost. Sensing this, the antelope doubled back without the hunter seeing him, and made his way to the hunter's house. When he got there he saw the poor owl had tried his best to help the turtle, but to no avail. The antelope reached up with his horns and carefully lifted the bag from the hook. Then the two of them scrabbled at the opening of the bag until the turtle was free. They all sighed and smiled at each other, three true friends.

They decided that living in the same part of the forest might be too dangerous now there was a hunter living close by. Sadly, the antelope took his family to a distant part of the forest, the owl flew with his family to some large trees in a different area, and the dear little turtle swam with his family to the far side of the lake. They never saw each other again, but I am sure that in their thoughts they remained true friends forever.

30

CARRYING A LOAD

This is a beautiful and well-known story in Buddhist tradition.

The monk and his student had journeyed together over many miles on their way to the capital. The student was in awe of his teacher and questioned him whenever he could about Buddhist teachings and scripture. The monk was only too glad to share his wisdom. It really was a journey of enlightenment for the young man.

After a few days of heavy rain, they came to a ford that was running deep with water. A difficult but necessary place to cross. As the two men began to roll up their gowns and make sure their bags were strung safely around their necks, they noticed a young woman standing at the edge of the ford. She was a delicate person, with clothes that were perhaps cut a little too low at the neckline; she wore makeup and painted her nails. The student turned up his nose at the sight of her. He had heard of such women. But to his amazement, his travelling companion went to speak to her, and finding she desperately needed to cross the river, invited her to climb onto his back. The monk steadied himself as he stepped into the deep water, using his staff to keep them both upright, and at last the two of them made it safely to the other side.

She carefully climbed from his back and thanked him greatly for his assistance. The monk nodded his head, rolled down his robes, said goodbye and carried on walking along the road. The student had made his way through the water, too, and after sorting out his robes he hurriedly took his place next to the monk. But as they walked, he was silent. All the questions he would normally have asked whirled around in his head.

How could such a woman ask for the help of a respected monk? How could the monk have spoken to such a woman, let alone carry her on his back? Why was he not filled with distaste because she had defiled his holy presence?

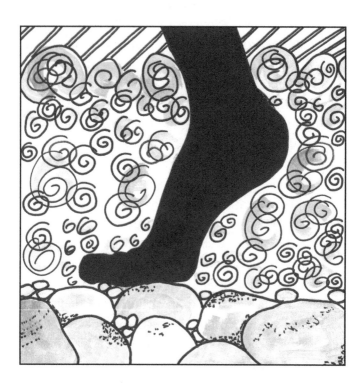

The thoughts got darker as he internalised his disgust. At last, he could bear it no longer and blurted out, 'Master, how could you defile yourself by helping such a woman?'

The monk did not even look at his student but kept walking.

'I seem to have been able to put down my load many miles ago, my boy, but you seem still to be carrying it with you.'

31

A Tail Tale

In a splendid castle there lived a king with his daughter, the princess. She was a sweet little thing, having everything she ever wanted, but, as such, she was rather spoilt. She did smile sometimes, but she also cried a lot when things didn't go her way.

One day, she woke up with a sore eye, and even though her father the king told her not to rub it, even though her nurse told her not to rub it, the sweet little thing rubbed it until it became an angry red. The king, of course, called for his physician, who was the best in the land. He told her not to rub it and then produced a little pot of ointment to rub gently on it. But as soon as she saw it, she screamed in anguish and refused to let him go anywhere near it. She carried on rubbing the eye and, of course, the worrying condition became worse and worse.

At last, in desperation, the king proclaimed a large reward for anyone who could cure his daughter. The very next day, a young man appeared, claiming to be a travelling physician. In fact, he was not even a doctor. He said that if he could examine the princess, he would be able to cure her.

So, he was admitted to her chamber, and with the king and the nurse watching anxiously, he began his thorough examination.

When he had finished, he stepped back and scratched his cheek. 'Mmm, oh dearie me.'

'What is it?' asked the king.

'Is it serious?' questioned the nurse.

'Whaaaaa!' cried the young girl. 'What is it?'

'Well, there is nothing much wrong with your eye but there is something else really quite serious.'

Again, the young princess burst into tears, yelling, 'What could be so serious?'

The young doctor thought for a moment, sucked in his breath and said, 'I am not sure I should tell you.' He looked at the king.

'Tell us what is wrong! Whatever it is, you *must* tell us!' the king implored.

At last the doctor nodded and began his diagnosis. 'Well, there is truly little wrong with the eye, that will get better in a few days, it is no problem. The big problem is that the princess will grow a tail, one of at least ten arms long. It may start growing very soon but if we can detect it as soon as it does begin to grow, we may be able to do something about it.'

Everyone was deeply concerned about this news. It was such serious news that the princess didn't cry but determined to take care of herself and look out for any signs of a tail appearing. She went to bed, rested, kept warm, drank and ate sensibly, and after a few days ... the eye problem had cleared as she was more concerned about the imminent tail.

The young doctor was sent for once again. He claimed his reward for curing the eye problem and had to admit the tail tale was just that – a tale.

Sometimes we can concentrate too much on the little things in life.

32

IT STARTED
WITH A DREAM

This is a beautiful story, filled with imagery and visions.

The king and his queen stood, side by side, before their trusted wise men. They waited anxiously for their deliberations.

Around two and a half thousand years ago in a kingdom in northern India, an area that we now call Nepal, a young man had been chosen to lead the Sakya tribe as their king. His name was Suddhodana and his capital city was Kapilavatthu. The country was beset with troubles, and the new king set about creating a system of government that could benefit his people. In time, as the country settled, the people became more content and the country showed early signs of the green shoots of prosperity. Their young king became known as the 'King of Law', and he was respected by both nobility and commoners alike. The future looked promising.

At the same time, King Suddhodana began to create himself a royal palace. The first wife he married was the daughter of a king of a neighbouring country. She was called

Maha Maya. She was a young woman of extraordinary beauty, and she was also highly intelligent, pious, virtuous and talented.

The king married many other wives, too, but Queen Maha Maya was his first and most beloved. Many of the other wives gave birth to royal children, which brought joy to the king and the country, but he so longed for a child from Maha Maya.

One night, the queen was alone in her apartments. She lay on her bed, resting – the day had been hot and sultry. The delicate fabric of her curtains blew in the gentle breeze, the room was illuminated by a perfect full moon, and the scent of jasmine filled the air.

As she began to fall into a light sleep, the moonlight gradually became more intense, and through half-open eyes she saw four beautiful spirits, devas, each standing at a corner of her bed. They smiled at her, and reaching out their hands, they each took hold of a bed post. Immediately, the queen and her bed began to rise, and she was carried away by the four spirits to the shores of Lake Anotatta, high in the Himalayas.

The moon still shone its silver light, which now danced on the gentle waves of the lake, and a cool breeze blew along the shoreline. The devas took the queen by the hand and guided her down to the edge of the water. There, they respectfully undressed her and bathed her in the clear waters of the lake, drying her with the softest of fabric. They dressed her in heavenly clothing, combed her hair and anointed her with perfumes, finally filling her hair with flowers. They withdrew from her and she stood in the moonlight, drinking in the experience.

Suddenly, in the distance, she saw a huge white elephant approaching her. He was a magnificent animal, swaying to and fro as he came closer, a beautiful white lotus flower clasped in his trunk. The elephant began to circle her, slowly, like a hypnotic dance, once, twice, three times, and then, gently, he entered her womb through her right side.

The queen woke with a gasp. She was back in her room with the moonlight, the breeze and the jasmine, and there lying beside her on her bed, a beautiful, white lotus flower. As she slowly gathered her senses, she knew that she had received a great vision.

Gathering her robe around her, she ran through the corridors to her husband's rooms, and there, sitting with him, still unsure of every detail, she told him of her dream. He stood and rubbed his brow – a wondrous vision indeed. The image of a white elephant was a symbol of greatness in their country.

And so, the wise men were called for. The king instructed his wife to retell her dream to them so that they could understand and interpret for them, and as she did so, there was much nodding of heads.

The king and his queen stood, side by side, before their trusted wise men. They waited anxiously for their deliberations.

After much hushed discussion, the wisest of the men turned from the rest and approached his king and queen. The king reached to hold his wife's hand and they both stood silently.

The trusted man began by telling them that the vision was indeed one of huge importance and foretold much. The queen was now with child, as the four devas had chosen her to give birth to The Purest One. Their child would grow to be a leader of men.

The queen was overjoyed at the news and her husband held her tightly.

'There is more, master,' said the old man. 'When your son reaches manhood, he will encounter an important fork in the journey of his life, and whichever path he chooses will determine his, and our, future. He will be a leader of men. One path will direct him to lead this earthly kingdom, but if he chooses the other, it will direct him on a spiritual journey where he will be a leader of minds.'

The king and queen looked at each other and smiled the smile of all new expectant parents. They thanked their advisers for their help and sent them away. In their hearts they knew they were to be given a child destined for greatness of being.

A great celebration was organised to share the wonderful news of the queen's pregnancy. All the noblemen and their families were invited to the palace to share in the good news. Gifts of food and clothing were distributed to the populace, and everyone waited with eager anticipation for the birth of the prince.

Queen Maha Maya lived her life with purity for both herself and the child she was carrying. She had a healthy and joyful pregnancy and longed for the day the child would arrive.

Now, it was customary in those times for an expectant woman to return to the house of her father to give birth. As the due date approached, the king made detailed plans to prepare for the queen's journey back to Koliya and the palace she had grown up in. He sent soldiers and workers to clear and repair the roads so that his pregnant wife could have as smooth a journey as possible, and arrangements were made to guard the queen as she travelled.

The day of her departure arrived, and the king escorted his precious wife to the beautiful golden palanquin in which she was to travel, escorted by an entourage of soldiers, servants and waiting women. The king kissed his wife and bade her farewell. He knew that the next time he saw her she would be holding their child. The procession began to move forward and left the confines of the city walls.

The journey was straightforward, and the queen enjoyed her travels. There were crowds in each little village or hamlet to cheer her on, and the views of the mountains reminded her of her childhood growing up in Koliya. After a day of travelling, it had been arranged to camp out in a beautiful park not too far from the borders of her father's kingdom, so she would be refreshed by a good night's sleep before she entered the palace the next morning. The queen was helped out of her palanquin and she decided to go for a short walk whilst the royal tent was erected.

She had heard much of this royal parkland, Lambini Park, and she enjoyed her stroll amongst the trees. Her women soon wanted her to return to the camp, but she insisted on walking a little further. The sky was now ink black and a familiar full moon cast its clear silver light before them. She was enchanted by the shadows and the patches of moonlight and the way the hanging blooms of flowers seemed to glow. Night owls and moths fluttered in the air.

And as she walked, she reached upwards to catch a cascade of blooms in her hand to pull it towards her face so she could smell the perfume. She gasped loudly. Clutching the sides of her stomach, she yelled with the first obvious pains of childbirth, and fell to the ground. The women raced forward and caught her. The birth was imminent. Scarves and blankets were cast on the ground under the branches of a Sala tree, and the queen gave birth quickly, helped by her women.

Although it was quick, it was not an easy birth. The child was delivered, and that child would grow up to be the Buddha.

And it is said that as soon as he was born, in the light of that beautiful moon, he took seven steps across the grass, each step cushioned by a beautiful white lotus flower. Upon taking the seventh step, he stood with one hand on his hip and the other above his head, finger pointing high in the sky and proclaimed, 'I am chief of the world! Eldest am I in the world! Foremost am I in the world! This is the last birth. There is now no more coming to be.'

The queen and the child were carefully carried back to the camp where both could rest. Messages were sent to her father that she had given birth and she would return to her husband's palace.

Queen Maha Maya returned home next morning. Her husband greeted her with joy and peered lovingly at his longed-for child lying in her arms. He was named Siddhartha Gautama. Great celebrations began and the people were overjoyed at the news.

But the queen took no part in the celebrations. It was thought at first that she was tired from the journey and giving birth, and so she remained confined to her bed. But it

soon became obvious that all was not well. A few days later, the celebrations ceased, suddenly, with the sad news that the queen had died. It was thought that the stress of giving birth to such a great person as the Buddha was far too much for any mortal body to bear – a tragic cost.

The queen's younger sister took charge of the child and became his adoptive mother. She and the king provided everything they could for the child, and he lived his childhood in the confines of the palace walls. Everyone waited for that time when the fork in the road would appear and Siddhartha would have choices to make.

33

ONE GREY HAIR

(JATAKA 9)

How many of us have watched in the mirror for that first grey hair to appear? And when it did, did it matter? Life is too short to waste. Even a long life.

In a time long before our time, there were people who lived far longer than we do now. They lived for many thousands of years.

There was a young man who had lived for eighty-four thousand years, as a child and a crown prince. As this story begins, he had been king for eighty thousand years.

One day, the young king was having his hair cut by the royal barber. 'If you see just one grey hair on my head, you must tell me immediately,' he instructed the barber.

'Of course, your majesty,' said the barber.

Four thousand more years passed, and the king ruled wisely. But one day, as he was having his hair cut, the barber noticed one single grey hair growing on the king's head.

'Oh, my lord, I can see one grey hair growing on your head.'

The king said, 'If this is true, pull the hair out and place it in my hand.'

The barber reached for his silver tweezers and carefully plucked the single grey hair from the king's head. He placed it in the waiting, outstretched hand of the king.

Now, the king had many, many years left to live and rule his country, maybe as many as another eighty-four thousand, but the more he looked at the one single grey hair, the more terrified he became. Surely, this was a sign that he was growing old and that death must be just around the corner. He thought of how stupid he had been wasting most of his life. And now he was nearing death, he realised just how little he had done with his life. 'I have done nothing to get rid of greed and envy, to live without hating, and to clear my ignorance by learning the truth and becoming wise.'

The more he thought along these lines, the more panic-stricken he became, until at last he decided that he must give up the kingship, ordain as a monk and spend the rest of his life in dedicated meditation. He was so overjoyed at his decision that he rewarded the barber with an enormous yearly income.

The king called his family to him and addressed his oldest son. 'My boy, I have been informed by my barber that I have a grey hair growing on my head. I am growing old and I realise that I have enjoyed living the life of a king for long enough. When I die, I want to be reborn into heaven and enjoy the benefits of a heavenly life. It is time for you to take over the task of ruling the country, for I shall abdicate and train as a monk and spend my life living in the forest.'

When the people heard of the king's decision, they assembled at the palace to ask him why he was leaving them.

The king stood before them and held up the offending grey hair. 'My people, this grey hair shows me that I have passed through the first stages of my life, youth, middle age and old age, and I am approaching my end. This first grey hair was a messenger of death sitting on my head. Grey hairs are angels sent by the gods of death. It is a signal that I should be ordained this very day.'

His news caused the people great sadness, but he left the city to go to live in the forest and was ordained as a simple monk. And there he was happy, for over the years he studied and lived with the monks and discovered:

Loving kindness and the tender affection for all,
Feeling sympathy and pity for all those who suffer,
Feeling happiness for all those who are joyful, and,
Finding balance and calm, even in the face of difficulties
or troubles.

After eighty-four thousand years of meditating and practising these states as a humble monk, he died. He was reborn in the high heaven world, to live a life a million years long.

34

THE MISSING SON

Many years ago, I was a storyteller at a walking and story holiday in southern Spain. One night, I gave the participants a challenge to create their own story. I gave them each one phrase printed on a piece of paper. We had been to visit a Buddhist temple on our walk that day, so each phrase was a Buddhist quote. One couple had a phrase warning of the danger of hanging onto beliefs, even when new and compelling evidence to the contrary was presented. At the end of the evening, they told this story by the light of an open fire. It was spellbinding. They kindly gifted me the story.

The men had been away since early morning, collecting food for the village. They had left the women and children at home to care for the elderly. As they approached the village later that day, they could see flames burning and smell the acrid smoke. Dropping everything, they ran to the village and were horrified to find that everywhere the houses were burned to the ground and there were bodies lying where they had fallen, trying to escape. Desperately, each man ran to where his home had once stood. One man found the body of his dead wife and his elderly father, still barely alive, lying against a tree trunk. He was badly hurt and just managed to tell his son that bandits had arrived and had killed everyone they came across, stolen what they could and set fire to the houses.

'But where is my little boy? I can't find him anywhere!'

The old man could not tell him and sadly passed away in his arms.

All the men buried their dead. This man buried his wife, his father, and placed a memorial for his son, whom he presumed had been killed by the bandits or taken away. Over time, many of the men moved away from the village, unable to bear the

sadness that hung in the air, but the man decided to rebuild his home and stay near the graves of his family and honour them. He tended his fields through the day, working hard to overcome his grief, but at night, when darkness came to the village, he simply locked his door and sat in the darkness.

On one of those dark nights, after the door had been locked, there was knocking at his door.

From the darkness inside the man shouted, 'Who is it?' He still feared the return of more bandits.

It was his teenage son. The bandits had kidnapped him and kept him hostage as a slave, but after many years of working hard for them, he had managed to escape and find his way home.

'Father, it is me, your son, I've returned home.'

The man inside moaned. Who could be tormenting him with such wicked lies?

'I have no son; my boy died many years ago. Go away.'

The boy tried to reason with his father, but he could not be persuaded. He had lived with the belief that his son had died along with the rest of his family many years ago and he would not, could not, change his mind.

At last, the son gave up trying and wandered away from the village.

Because the father would not change his long-held beliefs, his truth, the two would never be reunited.

35

THE GARDENER
AND THE ANTELOPE

(JATAKA 14)

There was once a skilled gardener called Sanjaya, who worked in the garden of the king. The garden was a pleasure ground for the royal family, and they marvelled at the trees, fruits and flowers that the gardener tended. Sanjaya loved working in the garden – he understood the natural world well.

One day, whilst working in a shady area, he noticed a wind-antelope carefully sniffing around, but as soon as it spotted the gardener it dashed away to safety. It came back every day, and it became used to the gardener's presence, only darting for the shade if the gardener made a sudden or loud movement.

Every day, Sanjaya took flowers and fruits into the palace, and one day he was met by the king. The king smiled at him, congratulated him on the fine flowers and fruits and asked if he had seen anything special in the gardens recently. Sanjaya told him about the wind-antelope and the king asked him if he could catch it for him. Sanjaya said that if he had honey, he could lure the creature into the palace itself. And so, the king ordered he be given all the honey he needed.

The gentle gardener began by smearing honey on the patches of lush grass where the antelope ate. It liked the taste of the sweetness and came back, day after day, to graze on the newly sweetened grass. Sanjaya tried approaching the antelope, but it ran away at the sight of him. The gardener persisted. In time, the antelope became used to him and even began to eat honeyed grass from his hand. One day, Sanjaya strapped a gourd of honey to his shoulder and stuffed handfuls of grass into his belt. Taking some of the grass, he dipped it into the honey and dropped it on the ground as he made his way to the palace. The wind-antelope now trusted him and followed, enjoying the grass as they walked, until the gardener led him in through the wide palace doors, which were shut firmly closed after the animal entered. When the antelope looked up from his eating and saw the king and the other humans, it began tearing around the palace in absolute terror.

The king turned to his advisers and said, 'This jungle creature was so scared and wary of men that it would dart away at the sight of them and not return to the same spot in fear that a human would appear again. And yet, see how the lust for sweet honey has snared it in a palace of humans and now it is imprisoned. There is nothing so vile as lust.'

With that, he ordered the doors to be flung open, and the terrified creature hurtled to safety.

36

THE KING OF
THE MONKEYS

As Buddhism swept across the land towards the East, it encompassed many other religions and adopted some of their cultures, beliefs and practices. Here is a story from Japan that introduces the notion of many gods and goddesses and the Jade Emperor.

The King of the Monkeys sat on the very highest branch of the tallest tree in the forest and surveyed his kingdom. He straightened his little crown and peered into the distance, checking for any other monkeys straying into his domain. And, as he did so, he noticed again the beautiful and mysterious Jade Palace belonging to the emperor. He had often watched the gods and goddesses arriving at the palace at the end of their day, and as the forest grew darker, the lights from the palace windows illuminated an enticing world inside. The Jade Emperor had certainly created a wonderfully comfortable and elegant space for the deities to spend their evenings. It made the King of the Monkeys think. Why shouldn't he, the king of so many, be a part of this, too?

So, next day, when all the deities had departed to start their day doing whatever deities do during the day, the monkey swung through the trees and in through an open window, landing right at the feet of the Jade Emperor himself.

'Good morning, my fine young fellow, and what can I do for you this morning?' asked the emperor. He had often been delighted to see the monkey troup swinging through the trees.

The King of the Monkeys took off his crown and bowed to the emperor, then, standing tall and making quite a play of placing his crown on his head again, said, 'I am the King of the Monkeys and I rule an extensive nation. My people hold me in great esteem. I have observed the splendid deities spending their evenings here with you in the palace, and I would like to join them. As a deity, of course.'

The Jade Emperor hid his smile – he did not want to offend such a respected chap.

'You see yourself as a God, do you?'

The monkey nodded his head furiously and then stopped, gathered himself, stood tall, and replied with one, regal nod.

The Jade Emperor stroked his beard thoughtfully. He liked this little fellow and thought that the deities would enjoy his company, too.

'I am willing to give it careful thought Monkey King, but, of course, the others would have to be consulted first. May I suggest that you sit in that rather splendid chair over there and wait for them all to return home this evening? Then we can ask them.'

The King of the Monkeys turned to look at the chair. It did so look like a throne. He nodded again, turned, walked over to the chair and sat, summoning up every regal ounce of dignity that he could.

The emperor was impressed; the King of the Monkeys looked very dignified. The emperor bowed and left the room.

The little monkey sat regally in the chair for as long as he could, but soon got bored. Normally he would be swinging around in the trees, chasing his wives and eating fruit, not sitting for hours in an uncomfortable human chair. He began tapping his fingers on the arm of the chair, scratching under his armpits and looking around. He noticed a rather enticing gold chandelier hanging high above him and wonderful cords of silk dangling beside the curtains, and he was off. He climbed the curtain ties and leapt towards the branches of the chandelier. He used his legs and his tail to gain momentum, and began swinging backwards and forwards, finally leaping to the ground, skidding on the rugs and sending chairs scattering in different directions. He was having a wonderful time. He was just running across the immense, polished dining table, when the first of the deities began to arrive home. The Jade Palace was a refuge from their busy schedules and so they were not happy to see a wild monkey causing havoc and whooping around their home. When the emperor came into the room, he saw the devastation and looked at all the deities holding their hands up in horror. He caught the monkey in full jump and placed him on the throne-chair. The monkey quickly gathered himself and sat upright.

'I apologise for our little friend, his excitement of being here with you all has obviously overcome him. May I introduce you to a new applicant for the role of Monkey God?'

The deities responded with various comments that all basically amounted to 'no way'.

But the emperor calmed them with a raised palm of his hand.

'It is, of course, early days, but I do believe that, given a fair chance, this splendid fellow could make a fine addition to our ranks.'

Everyone recognised the stern tone in the emperor's voice and of course agreed.

The next day, the deities left on their missions. The emperor came into the throne room and looked at the eager monkey, who was determined to make this work. Perhaps some responsibility would help?

'I have seen you and your people climbing around in the tops of the trees. I would think that you know where all the best fruits grow?'

The monkey nodded his head.

'The favourite food of all the deities is apricots. Do you know where they grow?'

The monkey nodded even more furiously. They were his favourite food too – another sign he should join the league of deities.

'Excellent. I think a really good way to make an impression on your colleagues would be to collect them a whole dish of the most delicious apricots. I am sure they would love that.'

The monkey's eyes opened wide with excitement at such a simple task to make a good impression. The emperor gave him a large basket to collect the fruits in and indicated a large, highly polished silver platter to present them on. The monkey grabbed the basket and sprang out of the window and across the tree canopy. Others from his tribe joined him, and when they arrived at the best apricot trees they all began gathering the fruits. They were so ripe and tasty that they had to try some themselves. The juice was so fragrant that wasps and other insects had begun to eat and burrow into the fruits as well. The King of the Monkeys made sure that some of the apricots went into the basket to fulfil his task.

As the sun began to set in the sky, the King of the Monkeys tore himself away from his helpers and, carrying the heavy basket, made his way back to the palace and in through the window. He sat on the table and began to take the apricots out of the basket and place them on the platter in as presentable a manner as possible. But some of the apricots, well, quite a lot of them, had grubs in them, so were squishy on one side. And even the most beautiful of specimens had claw or teeth marks in them. But the little fellow carefully arranged them in a beautiful pyramid shape.

When the deities arrived home, they eagerly waited for everyone to be assembled before they sampled the fruits. The emperor smiled at the monkey – all seemed well. At last, with many a 'thank you', the deities carefully selected a delicious fruit from the carefully arranged platter, only to find that it was too carefully arranged. Each fruit was full of insects, bruised beyond recognition or had bite marks or worse on their surface. Each deity threw back the disgusting fruit onto the platter, turning frantically to find something to wipe their hands of the sticky, over-ripe juice. Everyone turned to the emperor.

'No, he has to go. He just has to go!'

The emperor looked at the little monkey, who had lifted his shoulders and scrunched his face as if to say, 'Ooops!', and smiled. He had tried so hard to please the others.

'I shall give him one more chance, and' – looking at the monkey – 'only one more chance.'

The others groaned and turned away to flop into their favourite easy chair.

The next day, the emperor realised that he had to find something simple and time consuming in order to assist the monkey to be successful in impressing the deities. He had the servants gather all the brass, gold and silver ware and place it on the large dining table. There was a box containing polish and dusters. Surely even the King of the Monkeys could manage to spend the day polishing all these ornaments without making a mess of the task? The monkey seemed quite excited at the challenge, especially when it was pointed out how the gods and goddesses loved to see the lights of the candles and fires sparkling on the beautifully polished items.

The King of the Monkeys spent all day carefully burnishing the candlesticks, the goblets, the piles of knives, forks and spoons, and all the other trinkets. He left the huge platter from the day before to the very end – he was determined to make a wonderful job of that. The emperor popped his head around the door several times during the day and was relieved to see the monkey working hard and making a great effort to achieve success.

At last the King of the Monkeys started on the platter. The edges were intricate, and he had to poke his little fingers into the duster to get the polish into the crevices and then buffed up. At last he was on to the central panel of the dish, a fine, smooth surface of the highest-quality silver. With relish, he spread polish onto the panel and then began to burnish and shine. It was looking so beautiful, and he held it up to the last of the sunlight to admire his work. But he had shone the plate so well that it acted as a mirror. The monkey had never seen his reflection before, and whether he thought it was a scary monster or a rival looking back at him, we will never know, but without warning he let out the hugest of monkey screams. The deities were just returning and were greeted by the deafening shriek and horrifying sight of all the precious items being scattered over the room as the monkey exploded in terror, knocking everything to the ground, causing even more ear-splitting noises as goblets, knives and plates crashed to the floor.

The emperor came rushing into the room to see what was happening and was horrified to see the chaos caused by the monkey.

The deities all shouted that this was enough, that the palace was a place of refuge and calm for them, and that the monkey was causing the exact opposite. He had to go.

The emperor turned to the monkey and said, 'I am afraid we have given you many chances my little friend and you have failed at every one. It is time for you to go.' And he pointed at the door.

The little monkey looked from the emperor to the deities, who all pointed to the door as well ... and he lost his temper. In his mind he had worked hard to join the group. Yes, there had been a few problems, but nothing serious. And he told them so. And finally he added: 'I am the king of a large area with many subjects. They worship me as a king and as a god. I am as good as any one of you, perhaps better. I should be a god; in fact I should be the emperor; in fact I should be the Lord of the Universe!'

There was a moment's silence as everyone digested just what the monkey had said. He had not only said he was better than them, even better than the emperor, but that he should take the place of the Lord of the Universe, the Buddha himself. Outrageous! He had well and truly overstepped the mark this time, and the King of the Monkeys knew that himself.

He was faced with a barrage of red, angry faces, with everyone pointing at the door. The little monkey took off his crown, and, dragging it along the floor, shoulders down and tail drooping, he slowly made his way to the door. He did stop once and turned beseechingly, but was met with furious faces and more pointing. He turned back to the door and was just about to leave, when he bumped into someone just entering – the Buddha himself.

'Well, what is happening here, I wonder?' he asked kindly.

The little monkey cringed as the deities and even the emperor shouted out all the things that had happened and the monkey's outrageous comments. The Buddha signalled them to hush.

'Is this true, my noble friend?' The monkey nodded.

'And you have a desire to take my place as Lord of the Universe?'

The monkey nodded as he knew he had to be truthful.

'Very well. Let me see. Do you like a challenge little fellow?'

The monkey looked up, smiled and nodded again.

The Buddha continued. 'If you can find somewhere in the universe where I cannot see you, and prove it, I will allow you to take my place.'

There was a gasp from the deities and the monkey's mouth dropped open. But the Buddha had spoken.

'Will you accept the task?'

The monkey nodded enthusiastically.

'But if you fail, you must leave the palace and go back to your life in the forest.'

The monkey nodded again.

'Then go,' said the Buddha.

The little monkey firmly placed his crown on his head, leaped onto the windowsill and out into the trees. He sat for a moment and thought. Where could he go where the Lord Buddha, the most powerful of the powerful, would not be able to see him? And how could he prove that he had been there? Of course, he needed to get as far away as possible, to the very edge of the universe itself, to a secluded corner where the Buddha never went. And summoning up all his Monkey King powers, he flew through the air at the speed of light to the very edge of the universe, where he was sure the Buddha rarely came. When he was there, he looked around and it was desolate, not a soul in sight. He reached into his pocket and pulled out a large pen, and there, on the wall of the universe itself, to prove that he had been there, he wrote:

'The King of the Monkeys was here. Ha Ha!'

He took one more look around him to see if the Buddha was watching, straightened his crown and whizzed back to the palace, landing at the very feet of the Buddha.

'Well, do you think you have completed the challenge successfully?' asked the Buddha.

'I certainly have,' said the monkey confidently. And with the deities, the emperor and the Buddha listening to him, he proudly told them of what he had done.

'And then, with my own pen, to prove I had been there, I wrote on the wall of the universe …'

But before the monkey could tell them, the Buddha, the Lord of the Universe, uncurled his hand so they could all see his palm, and there, written in shaky lettering, was:

'The King of the Monkeys was here. Ha Ha!'

Everyone turned to the monkey and raised their eyebrows. The monkey jumped onto the windowsill and with a final 'Ha Ha!' leapt into the trees, never to be seen in the palace again.

37

THE SACRIFICE

(JATAKA 50)

Once there was a kingdom with a wise and fair king. The country was prosperous and peaceful, and the king was loved by his people. Other rulers bowed down to him. He worked solely for the good of his people, and the land was free of disturbances, disasters and disruption.

However, one year the country was hit by a devastating drought, and whether this was due to the laziness of the people or an oversight of the gods to send rain, it caused the king great concern. He was sure that it must have something to do with him, and so he called a meeting of his advisers and religious leaders to ask them if they could instruct him what to do. They were experts at ritual, and after spending some time discussing and arguing, they assembled before the king and told him that he should sacrifice a thousand animals. This would appease the gods and encourage them to send rain. The king was not sure how this could help, and he was not pleased at the thought of hurting so many animals. He did not want to offend the elders and so he amended their advice a little.

He told them his plan. Yes, a sacrifice was needed, but he would sacrifice a thousand humans instead. Only citizens who had caused wrongs, were lazy or neglected the land would be chosen, and there would be a team of watchers, looking out for anyone who was a danger to the country or strayed from the path of goodness.

The people behaved well. Children obeyed their parents and their teachers. The adults became more respectful and kinder, working hard on the land and sharing their good fortune with those who had little.

And the king showed the true meaning of sacrifice. He set up assembly rooms throughout the land and there he gave away amounts of his own wealth to those who needed help to prosper. The country flourished as poverty died away, and the kingdom entered a golden age.

And, of course, the thousand human sacrifices were never made.

38

A Head and Tail Tale

Have you ever seen the marks in the desert sand that a winding snake makes as it scurries across the burning surface? A true beauty of nature and something that has existed since time began. A natural motion honed and practised.

Well, one day, a snake had just side-winded, twisted and turned and darted from the scrub to the shade of the village wall. It lay, still, calm and safe, when suddenly the tail of the snake said to the head of the snake: '*I* should be the one to lead the way. At least, some of the time.'

The snake's head turned and looked at his tail disdainfully. 'But I have always been the one to lead the way and decide on our direction. Why have you suddenly decided that you should do it?'

And with that, he threw his head forward, and ignoring his tail's request, began to move along the bottom of the wall, keeping in the cool shade.

But the tail was having none of this, and quickly wound himself around the stem of a bush, refusing to wriggle a wiggle further. The snake's head tried to ignore his tail and pulled

with all his might, but he just couldn't shift his rear end, and in the end they both collapsed on the sand in exhaustion.

Finally, the head decided to give in to the tail's request and told him he could set the course, if he so wished.

The tail was beside himself with excitement and shouted with glee, 'At last! I'm the leader for a change!'

And even though he was exhausted from the struggle, he set off on a new path, totally forgetting that he had no eyes with which to see the road ahead and no experience of leading. Without an inkling of what lay ahead, he slid across the road, just as a heavy lorry passed by.

39

THE HONOURED GUEST

It is good to find a story set in current times to join the collection.

The small monastery, down a side street in New York, had built up quite a community of followers, and the American monks were well respected in their teachings, their devotion to the community and their connections to the Buddhist centres in the East. All the monks had studied in South Asia and travelled whenever they could to monastic places of education. They built up their knowledge to pass on to their followers.

And there was great excitement in the community as one of the greatest teachers in northern India was coming to spend time at their monastery as he toured parts of America.

Their honoured guest was due to arrive on the Friday and during the time leading up to that day everyone was involved in making the monastery building as beautiful and as clean as they could. On the Thursday, all the vacuum cleaners, mops and buckets, and dusters were earning their keep.

But unbeknown to the community, their honoured guest had arrived early, and here he was, standing at the front door, bemused by this hive of activity.

'What is everyone doing?' he asked a woman who was frantically sweeping the front steps.

She began to hurriedly and excitedly tell him about who was coming, how they were expecting their honoured guest the next day and how they were preparing for his visit so thoroughly, when suddenly she realised who she was talking to and trailed off into silence.

'Well, if everyone is working so hard for my visit tomorrow, we had better get a move on.'

And, putting his case on the ground and rolling up the sleeves of his gown, he dunked a cloth into a bucket of hot, foamy water, dropped to his knees and began to clean the ironware at the sides of the steps.

40

THE WALKING STICK – A FOLK TALE FOR THE FUTURE

The following piece is not a folk tale, as yet. It is an account of the death of the thirteenth Dalai Lama and the search for his successor. It is full of historical data and yet laced with Tibetan beliefs that give the account that other-worldly feel that I am sure will make the story a much-loved folk tale in the near future.

High in the hills in the north-east of the country, a farmer, Choekyong Tsering, rode back to his farmhouse in Taktser, to tell his family and workers the news he had heard in the market that day. The sad death of the Dalai Lama would throw his wife and four children into deep mourning, but little did they realise just how this news would profoundly affect their family.

At the very end of 1933, in the tenth month of the Water Bird, the whole nation of Tibet was plunged into deep shock and disbelief. The thirteenth Dalai Lama, the secular and spiritual leader of Tibet, Thubten Gyatso, had died after a short illness, at the age of fifty-eight.

Considered to have been one of the greatest Dalai Lamas, his death would have a huge effect on the country and its people. He had ruled Tibet since 1895, and in those thirty-eight years he had modernised much of the state in order to combat the rise of neighbouring China. In 1911, when China revolted against their emperor, he lost no time in declaring Tibet's independence from China. Persuading the monastic and aristocratic powerhouses in the country to work with him, he set about a long list of reforms. He extended education, introduced a postal service with telegraph and telephone systems, and made taxation fairer. He reformed the penal system and abolished capital punishment, and he set up a small military force along British lines. The Dalai Lama was determined that the small nation was prepared to meet anything modern times threw at them, especially the rise of Red China.

Only two years before his death, he had caused consternation in the country talking about the rise of communism and the threats it could pose to their 'spiritual and cultural conditions'. A people with the notion that the surrounding mountains would protect them from any external threat now began to pay more attention to the rising power on their doorstep.

The death of their leader caused huge and personal grief to the people of Lhasa and the surrounding country. Theirs was a deeply religious culture, and whole families and villages went into mourning, weeping openly in the streets. Solemn drums beat out funereal sounds from the palace rooftops and all decorations and prayer flags were removed. The people wore traditional dark mourning clothes, with no jewellery or embellishments, and dancing and singing were forbidden. Simple lamps burned in the darkness of evening and prayers were offered at the temples and home altars.

After the traditional period of forty-nine days of mourning had been observed, normality resumed. Work and family life began again, but there was an emptiness in the land. The main question on everyone's mind was, 'Will he return to us soon?'

Throughout the country, thoughts were turned to when and how the Dalai Lama's reincarnation would be found. Each Dalai Lama has the power to choose where and to whom he will be reborn.

> For as long as space endures,
> And for as long as living beings remain,
> Until then may I, too, abide
> To dispel the misery of the world.

The Taktser house was a largish farmhouse and had belonged to the family for many generations. They had farmed in the uplands of Amdo, growing mainly wheat and barley, and vegetables like peas, potatoes, onions, turnips and radishes. They drank butter tea and barley beer. They worked hard and lived simply. The village was spread out, with strips of land separating the houses. Each house had a stone wall built around it and large dogs could roam free inside during the hours of darkness. Religion played a great part in the villagers' lives, and the children would even sometimes play at building temples. Monks regularly visited the houses for alms and to bless the families. The village was surrounded by mountains, and these played a great part in their everyday lives. They built little piles of stones to represent the peaks, and laid flowers and offerings to the mountain deities. This part of the country was seen as the cradle of Tibetan culture but families from China had long been migrating to this rich land to settle.

The role of Dalai Lama is not an ancient concept, only starting in the sixteenth century when Tibet was experiencing an important and successful period. The first five Dalai Lamas ruled effectively but after that no Dalai Lama ruled Tibet for more than a few years. These men were all discovered at extremely young ages, too young to rule in their own right, so a regent was placed to rule in their stead until they were around eighteen years of age. Having taken their rightful position, they died soon after. Of all the Dalai Lamas from the fifth to the thirteenth, only one reached maturity. It is presumed they were poisoned by the reigning regents, who had become accustomed to the power and authority their role had given them. The thirteenth Dalai Lama survived an attempt on his life when he was twenty-two. The case became known as the 'case of the accursed shoes', as the retiring regent attempted to take power from the young man using black magic. Some sort of magic incantation was placed in the sole of the Dalai Lama's new boots, and when this was discovered the young ruler soon suspected that an attempt on his life had taken place. The ex-regent was implicated in the crime. He was placed under house arrest and, mysteriously, he, too, soon died.

So, the sudden death of the thirteenth Dalai Lama, who had seemingly experienced a mere cold-like illness, caused concern and panic in all. A young monk, a favourite of the late ruler and tipped to be the next regent, was suspected of foul play, placed under house arrest and swiftly exiled from the country. Then began the struggle to appoint a new regent. The powerful families and monastic traditions began vying for their candidate to take the position, and there was great concern that officials from the Chinese government might infiltrate the selection process. At last, a young and inexperienced monk was chosen in haste. Named Reting, he unfortunately would allow all the wonderful reforms of the thirteenth Dalai Lama to crumble to nothing. The economy would become almost bankrupt, ethical standards would slip and the hoped-for bright future of the country would disappear.

But two urgent tasks faced the new regent: to build a splendid golden mausoleum in memory of the ex-ruler and, most important of all, to find the reincarnated successor to the late leader.

Many young couples and families would give birth to male children in the next few months and years, and wonder if their child possessed the spiritual consciousness of the late leader. Would they be parents of the chosen one?

The succession of Dalai Lama is neither hereditary nor elective but an act of reincarnation, and the search begins within about a year of the former ruler's death. The age of the boy-child would be unknown, and his whereabouts would be decided by divination of the signs. He would have certain bodily characteristics and possess remarkable spiritual and mental attributes.

And so, a year after the death, the government began its official search. A proclamation was issued instructing the local authorities to keep a look-out for any special children, especially those that displayed the physical characteristics of the recently deceased Dalai Lama: 'The skin of the legs ought to be striped as a tiger's; the eyes wide and the brows turned outwards; the ears large; two fleshy excrescences should be found near the shoulder blades, as is token of the two extra arms of Chenrezig, the god whose earthly embodiment the Dalai Lama is supposed to be; last, the palms should bear the pattern of a seashell.'

The embalmed body had been placed respectfully on a throne on a wooden dais in preparation for the people of Lhasa to file past, paying their respects to their dearly departed leader. Many were expected to attend. The body was sitting crossed legged and dressed in gold brocade, facing towards the south. White scarves were offered in homage by the passing mourners. At the end of the day, when the crowds had disappeared, the attendants noticed that the head of the body had turned slightly, towards the north-east. They thought this was a result of the heat and gently returned the head to its original position, but after a second day, the head was found to have turned again. Was this a sign that the reincarnation was to be revealed in the north-east of the country?

Over the next few months, a series of omens seemed to back up this theory. A patch of snapdragons grew from the north-eastern side of the dais where public sermons took place; a giant star-shaped fungus grew on the north-eastern pillar of the shrine where the Dalai Lama's tomb was being constructed. Strange cloud formations with rainbows through them appeared in the sky above the mountains to the north-east. Such signs were important to the people and made perfect sense to them.

The next two years passed without any encouraging news.

In 1935, Regent Reting and a group of his most trusted officials journeyed into the mountains to visit a sacred lake, Lhamoi Lhatso. It was said that the lake and its surroundings encouraged visions and prophecies. In fact it was here that the whereabouts of the previous Dalai Lama had been proclaimed. Whilst there, the still, deep blue waters created visions for some and nothing for others. The regent had a vision, but for some reason did not share this for a whole year, in the meantime pondering on what it had meant. Eventually, he announced to his Assembly that he had seen three Tibetan letters, a monastery with roofs of jade green and gold, a twisting road leading eastward to a bare pagoda-shaped hill, and a small, one-storey house with oddly shaped guttering and turquoise roof tiles. He was now sure that the first letter, Ah, stood for the province of Amdo in the north-east, a large province populated mainly by Tibetans but ruled by a Muslim warlord in the name of Nationalist China.

This news caused consternation in the government. It was felt to be unwise to be searching in this sensitive area. And so, three search parties were sent secretly into the region. Each one was led by a prominent Lama, supported by monks and lay government officials. Their mission was to identify any young boys who were considered special and bore a physical resemblance to the previous Dalai Lama. It would be a difficult and arduous journey, no doubt taking several years. Their search must evade the Chinese agents working in the area and yet be thorough.

Life in the little village of Taktser continued. Choekyong Tsering's family had changed a little. Two of his sons had joined the priesthood at the local monastery and they had a new son, Lhamo Dhondup, now two years old, running around the farm. The little boy was a vibrant child and made quite an impression with the monks when visiting his brothers at the monastery. So much so, that his name was put forward as a child worth considering in the search for the new Dalai Lama.

Three children had been seriously noted by the chief Lama at Kumbum Monastery in Amdo and therefore the search parties decided that they must visit. There was a delay in setting off because of heavy snowstorms but at last a party of men arrived at the monastery, relieved to see that it was a three-tiered pagoda-styled building with the jade green and gold roofs of the regent's vision.

Kesang Rinpoche led the mission to visit the boy in Taktser. It was difficult journeying during the winter months but at last they neared the village. They had decided to pose as a group of traders, and when they reached the farm Kesang Rinpoche would dress as a servant so that he could easily access the kitchen where the child would be. Meanwhile, his servant would pretend to be in charge.

Their hearts sang as they approached even nearer, as there, rising high above the village, was the pagoda-shaped mountain and, in its shadow, lay a single-storey house with turquoise tiles and strange guttering made of gnarled juniper branches. Prayer flags fluttered from the gateposts.

The 'leader' was taken straight into the house and the 'servant' made his way into the kitchen, where a small boy was playing on the floor. As soon as the child looked up, he ran to Kesang Rinpoche and climbed on his knee. The 'servant' was wearing typical travelling clothes but around his neck he had a string of rosary beads that had belonged to the thirteenth Dalai Lama. The little boy seemed to recognise them and indicated that he would like to wear them. He was asked various questions about the group of traders and the little child knew their real names.

The traders stayed the night but went on their way the next morning, asking if they could call in the next time they were passing.

Meanwhile, the visits to the other children had not gone to plan. One had unfortunately died and the other screamed in terror when visited – judged not to be the behaviour of an imminent Dalai Lama. And so, every effort was to be put into the examination of the Taktser child.

A few weeks later, a large party of dignitaries and servants set off for Taktser village. They eventually arrived at the farmhouse in the afternoon. The farmer and his wife were amazed at the grandeur of the visiting group. They had begun to wonder if their son was more than special. They noticed that the leader of the group had been a servant before and the leader was now a servant, which caused them confusion. It was not long before the leader informed the parents that the visitors hoped their child was the true incarnation of the departed Dalai Lama, and would they allow them to carry out some tests? Permission was gladly given, and several of the party went with the parents into the kitchen, where once again the child was playing. The boy's face lit up with a smile when he saw his friend back at the house again.

The tests given had been tried and tested over the centuries. The child was expected to remember objects and people that the late Dalai Lama would have owned and known. Also, he would be able to recite sacred texts that a child of that age would not have heard before.

Pairs of articles were laid out on the kitchen table and the child asked to choose from them. There were two black and two yellow rosaries – he chose the two that had belonged to the late ruler. They next presented to him two walking sticks: one had belonged to the Dalai Lama, the other to Kesang Rinpoche himself. The child first touched Kesang's stick but then changed his mind and took the correct one. When the group considered this near miss, it was suddenly realised that in fact both walking sticks had belonged to the Dalai Lama, but he had given one to Kesang as a gift many years ago. They next gave him the choice of two drums, one of which was used by the late ruler to summon his servants. The drum belonging to the Dalai Lama was very plain and simple, whereas the other was brightly coloured with tassels. A child would normally have been attracted to the brightness of the incorrect drum, but he took the simple one and immediately began to play it expertly. Indeed, when it was time for bed, no amount of coaxing could persuade the usually biddable child to give back the drum, and so he was allowed to keep it.

The search party were sure that they had found the correct child. He even had the signature tiger-striped skin on his legs and unusually large ears. A coded message was sent to Lhasa. It was decided that to evade the Chinese spies, it would be announced that several possibilities had been discovered and a decision would be made from these. When the group left the farmhouse, soldiers were stationed to guard the family.

Several days later, the two-year-old child and his parents were taken to Kumbum Monastery in preparation for the journey to the capital. But the parents would leave the monastery to make their way back to their farmhouse. Only Lhama Dhondup would travel on to the capital. His brief childhood was already over.

CROSSING TO
THE OTHER SIDE

The first time I read this story, I laughed out loud. The sign of a great story – so wise and yet so comical.

The young Buddhist monk was exhausted as he made his way back home to the monastery where he had lived and studied for so many years. He had been away for months, teaching in another province, and although he had enjoyed his time away, he so relished the thought of being home, amongst his teachers and his friends. But the journey had not been easy. The weather had been atrocious, and he had had to battle his way through heavy rain and fierce winds. At last he was in sight of the monastery on the hill, and he was rewarded for his arduous journey with a beautiful burst of sunlight. He smiled as he made his way down to the river where he would be able to cross by using the stepping stones, over which he had many a time carefully picked his way. But to his horror he found that the heavy rains had swelled the river so much that the stepping stones were nowhere to be seen in the now torrential river. He frantically looked up- and downstream for some other way to cross but

he knew very well there were no bridges on this stretch of river. In desperation, he looked across at the monastery, now so close, and noticed that the head monk was sitting on a rock on the opposite bank, reading a book in the sun.

'Master, Master!' shouted the young man, waving his arms above his head.

The head monk put down his book and smiled at the young man.

'Master, can you tell me how to get to the other side?'

The head monk thought for a second and shouted back across the river, 'You're already there my boy, you're already there.'

Story Synopses

1 Wild Strawberries. A man escaping a tiger falls down a ravine, only to have his fall broken by a vine. Above him stands the tiger, below him, its mate, and a mouse has begun to chew through the vine. He picks a wild strawberry that tastes so sweet.

2 The Talkative Turtle. A turtle who never stops talking comes up with a disastrous plan to fly with the birds.

3 Maybe. An old man answers simply, 'Maybe' to all the statements made by his neighbours.

4 A Favourite Tree. A hunter hides in the branches of a tree where an antelope regularly feeds on fallen fruit. In his desperation to lure the wary antelope closer to the tree so that he can snare him, he throws fruit towards the animal. The antelope decides that if the tree can behave out of character, then he will, too, and bounds off to feed somewhere else.

5 Muddied Water. The Buddha sends one of his young, inexperienced followers down to the river to collect water. The young man finds the water is muddy due to animals crossing through it, so does not collect any. Buddha sends him back several times until at last the young man finds that the water has cleared. Sometimes we need to let things settle before becoming involved.

6 The King and the Tortoise. A king who is becoming lethargic in the governance of his country is introduced to a wise but slow-moving tortoise by a concerned adviser. Through listening to the tortoise, the king mends his ways.

7 The New Buddha. The students at a monastery are challenged to collect precious metals by hard work rather than begging, to be melted down and create a new statue of Buddha. One young storyteller is anxious to be the best, but makes one huge mistake in not accepting a copper coin from a servant. The statue is flawed, and he eventually realises it is because of his error. As soon as he rectifies his mistake, the statue emerges from the mould, perfect. Similar story to 'The Widow's Mite'.

8 Fresh Breath. A devout king notices that the breath of a visiting young monk is delightfully fragranced. He discovers that in a past life the young man was a follower of Buddha, speaking eloquently and beautifully of him. In every incarnation since then, the young man's breath has had this delightful fragrance, uplifting all those that listen to his teachings.

9 The Miser. A greedy, rich man loves the taste of lamb and persuades his sons to create an altar to a tree on their land that he assures them is sacred. They do this, and regularly slaughter a lamb to honour the gods in the tree. The miser dines well on lamb that he doesn't have to pay for. After many years, the miser dies, is reincarnated as a lamb in the family's flock and is about to be slaughtered as an offering. Fortunately, a wise man is passing by and realises that the lamb is the incarnation of the father. The offering is saved, and the sons decide never to slaughter an animal ever again.

10 Mother Love. A mother elephant and her calf have the perfect, loving relationship. As the calf grows, he becomes the most handsome of pure white elephants, but he still cares for his now old and blind mother. A local king has the white elephant captured and brought to the palace, and although the creature is well cared for, he will neither eat nor drink and slowly fades. The king at last asks the elephant why he is not happy, and he tells him of his mother, now alone in the wild. The king takes pity and releases him. The elephant runs back to his mother, finds her at death's door, but, through his care, restores her health.

11 The Worm. Two monks who are lifelong friends die within a few days of each other. One of the monks passes on to the heavenly realms, but he can't find his friend. He discovers that he has returned as a worm in a dung heap. He tries to rescue his old friend but the worm will not come with him – he enjoys living in his dung heap.

12 Choosing a Tree. A new king wants to ensure everyone in his kingdom lives a safe life, including the tree fairies. He asks them to choose a tree or plant to make their home in. Some stay together and make their homes in trees and plants in the forest where there is safety in numbers, whilst others decide to make their homes in large trees that stand alone. When a storm comes, the fairies in the forest are safe, whereas the fairies in the individual trees are in danger, for these solo trees cannot bend with the winds and are uprooted. All the fairies go to live in the forest.

13 The Need to Win. The king of a certain country is determined that his kingdom and citizens be the best at everything. An archery competition in a neighbouring country means he has to find the best archers, but his search is in vain. He stumbles across a simple farm worker who at first seems to be the best archer he has encountered – but no. After their meeting, the king changes his view on life, to the benefit of himself and his people.

14 The Rich Man. An obviously rich nobleman is crossing an icy road when he slips and crashes to the ground. His heavy jewellery weighs him down and he cannot get up. All the passers-by pass by until a Buddhist monk approaches and happily lies down beside him.

15 Crossing the Desert. An experienced young merchant is leading a large caravan of wagons across a difficult desert. On the last evening, when they make camp, he tells his men to get rid of all the water barrels and boxes of food, as they will not need them on the final stage of the journey, and their journey will be easier without this heavy load. However, as they travel through that last night, the pilot guiding them in the first wagon falls asleep and somehow the oxen turn round and make their way back into the worst part of the desert. When the merchant realises what has happened, he worries that his men and animals will die of thirst. He notices a clump of grass growing and orders the men to dig under it, sure that water is below it. The men dig for a while but give up hope, especially when they come to a slab of rock. As they walk away, the merchant orders a young lad to smash the rock and, sure enough, they find water beneath it. Experience and faith pay off.

16 Grandma's Blackie. A poor, old woman adopts a calf and cares for him as dearly as her child. She calls him Blackie. He soon grows into a large bull, but the old woman still works hard to care for him. He decides he must help *her* for a change. One day a caravan of five hundred wagons comes through the village but cannot cross the river as it is swollen. The bull offers to help, and the caravan master offers him two golden coins for each wagon. It is hard work, but he soon drags all five hundred carts safely across. The merchant gives him a bag of coins, but Grandma's Blackie realises that the merchant has short-changed him and will not move out of the way of the first wagon. The merchant realises that the bull is intelligent and gives him the full amount. The old woman is astounded at the bag of coins but says there was no need for him to work for her; he is her child and she must provide for him, always. They live happily together.

17 The Wooden Bowl. An old father comes to live out his days with his son and daughter-in-law. He helps where he can and looks after his only grandchild, too. But, over the years he becomes infirm. He cannot help around the farm and soon needs care himself, causing his son and his wife more work. They become annoyed with him, especially when he breaks a pottery plate, and so give him a wooden bowl from the farm to eat from. They make him sit in the corner, out of the way. One day the farmer sees his son carving some wood, making wooden bowls for when the parents grow old. The farmer and his wife bring their father to the table and give him a pottery plate – the respect he deserves. Out of the mouths of babes.

18 The Golden Mallard. A father dies, leaving his wife and daughters in dire financial straits. However, his next life is as a mallard, and one that has golden feathers. He flies to their aid, offering a feather whenever he visits, and they become financially secure. But the wife becomes greedy and decides on one visit to pluck all the feathers at once … but they don't grow back golden. The mallard escapes and never returns.

19 The Glorious Stag. A herd of deer is led by a magnificent stag, who keeps his herd safe. He rescues a drowning man from the river, and the only reward he asks for is that the man doesn't tell anyone about them. The man hears that the queen had dreamt about the stag and wants to own it – a large reward has been offered. The man tells the king of the stag's whereabouts. The stag stops the king from shooting him and tells him the story of the drowning man. The king is appalled with the man. The stag persuades the king and his people to give up hurting animals.

20 East and West. Original story. An imagined story giving an alternative storyline to the life of Jesus.

21 The Noise the Hare Heard. A sleeping hare is woken by the noise of ripe fruit dropping. Thinking the earth is ending, he runs to escape, gathering others as he runs. A lion stops them, finds the real reason for the noise, and the animals return to the forest. Similar theme to 'Chicken Licken'.

22 Thief! A monk who has just completed a long period of fasting is invited into a couple's home for food. They take so long to serve up the food that the monk can wait no longer, and whilst they are out of the room he reaches for something to eat. Distraught at what he has done, he accuses his right hand of being a thief.

23 The Selfless Hare. Four animal friends live in the forest, and their leader, the hare, encourages them to be kind to travellers. One of the gods decides to test them, appears as a poor traveller and asks for food. The three other animals all give him the food they have collected for their own meals …

but the hare only has grass. Instead, he attempts to sacrifice himself, by throwing himself on a fire to cook. Fortunately, the god swiftly stops this and rewards the hare by inscribing the surface of the moon with the image of the hare.

24 The King of the Water Buffalo. A naughty monkey watches how all the buffalo are calm and gentle and respectful of their king. He becomes jealous and makes several attacks with words and stones, but none of the water buffalo responds. A tree god asks why the king has not reprimanded or attacked the monkey. 'Cause and effect,' says the king. Everything we do has a consequence.

25 The Seven Princes. A worried king suspects that any one of his seven sons could kill him and claim the throne, and so he banishes all seven along with their wives. The oldest son and his wife survive their ordeal in the forest, whereas the wives of the other sons do not. The couple live in a hut at the side of a river, and one day save a severely disabled man from drowning. The wife falls in love with this man and attempts to kill her husband by pushing him off a cliff. But he survives and escapes back to the city of his birth. He claims the throne, now his father has died. His wife and her lover come to the city to beg. The king sees her and makes a spectacle of her before the people. Her punishment is not pleasant.

26 The Tiger's Whisker. A newly married couple are separated by war. When the husband returns, he is a changed man. A wise man says he can help cure her husband, but she must provide an ingredient for the cure: a whisker from a tiger. She spends months befriending a tiger until one day she can pluck a whisker from his nose. The wise man begins to create the potion but drops the whisker into the fire.

The woman is distraught, but he assures her that if she can befriend and calm a ferocious tiger with patience, then she can do the same with her disturbed husband.

27 The Mustard Seed. A distraught woman approaches the Buddha asking for help as her baby has died. The Buddha asks her to go to householders in the village and get a mustard seed from those who have never experienced death. She visits every house but, at the end of the day, has no mustard seeds. She realises that death is a part of everyone's life.

28 The Goblins and the Merchants. Two merchants, one experienced, the other not, are due to make the same journey. It is decided that they should go at different times. The inexperienced merchant goes first but en route is met by a group of goblins in disguise. The goblins persuade the travellers to ditch their heavy water jars as there is plenty of water ahead, and storms. The travellers do this but soon find out about the lie. Weakened by thirst, they are easy prey for the goblins, who kill and eat them. When the experienced merchant meets the same group of goblins, again in disguise, he refuses to believe their lies and survives the desert crossing.

29 Three Friends. Three animal friends meet regularly in the forest but are hunted by a hunter. All three help each other to escape from the hunter and, in the end, move to a different part of the forest to live safely. Reminiscent of 'The Lion and the Mouse' story.

30 Carrying the Load. A respected monk carries a young woman across a deep ford. His younger travelling companion is appalled that he would associate himself with a woman in such a way, but the wise man tells him not to over-think the situation and carries on the journey.

31 A Tail Tale. The king's daughter is spoilt and when she develops a sore eye, she screams and refuses to allow anyone near her. The king offers a reward to anyone who can help. A young man comes forward and says the eye problem is nothing, but worryingly, she has another ailment – she will soon grow a tail. The young princess is so concerned that she looks after herself; she sleeps, eats, keeps warm and keeps an eye open for the appearance of a tail. The sore eye, of course, heals quickly and when the young man collects his reward he confesses that the tail tale was an untruth. Sometimes we can concentrate too much on the small things in life.

32 It Started with a Dream. The king and queen wish dearly for a son. The queen has a vision that foretells of a child being born. The boy child is born whilst the queen is travelling to her father's palace. He is Buddha. The huge celebrations are curtailed by the news that the queen has passed away.

33 One Grey Hair. A king who lives in a time where everyone lives thousands of years is terrified when his barber finds one grey hair. The king decides that he must be near the end of his life. As his death will soon come, he tells his son and the people that he will abdicate and live the life of a monk for what time he has left. Everyone is sad. The king goes off and lives for thousands of years as a monk.

34 The Missing Son. The men of the village go off hunting and when they return they find the village has been attacked and all the women and children have been killed. One man carries on living in his house alone. One night, when the door has been bolted, he hears knocking from someone claiming to be his son. The boy had been kidnapped during the attack but has managed to escape. The father will not listen, believing it is someone playing tricks. He sends the young man away without even seeing him.

35 The Gardener and the Antelope. The king's gardener tells the king about a beautiful wind-antelope that visits the garden. The king asks if he can catch it. The gardener entices the antelope with honey and one day tricks it into following him into the palace. The king is amazed how something could be lured into danger so easily and blames lust. He lets the antelope go free.

36 The King of the Monkeys. The King of the Monkeys decides that he would like to become a deity and live with the other gods in the Jade Palace. The Jade Emperor gives him many chances to prove himself, but he fails every test. The petulant monkey states that he is as good as any of the other deities, perhaps even better, and he wants to be the Lord of the Universe ... the Buddha himself. The Buddha hears of this and sets the monkey one more challenge: to find a hiding place that cannot be found by the Buddha. Again, the monkey fails and contents himself with going back to being the King of the Monkeys in the forest.

37 The Sacrifice. There are worrying times in the kingdom – a drought – and the king wants to know the reason for it and how it can be rectified. His advisers say that he must sacrifice a thousand animals. The king is not happy about this but does not want to offend his advisers, so he changes their advice a little. He says that he will sacrifice a thousand humans but only those who cause problems or are lazy. Everyone works hard and is polite and thoughtful, to prove they should not be the ones to be sacrificed. The kingdom flourishes. There was no need for any sacrifice of lives.

38 A Head and Tail Tale. The tail of a snake suddenly decides that he wants to lead the way, and the head reluctantly agrees. But they have forgotten that the tail has no vision or experience of leading.

39 The Honoured Guest. A New York Buddhist monastery is expecting a visit from a great teacher from the East. Everyone is making ready for the visit by cleaning everywhere. The guest arrives unexpectedly a day early, and when he hears everyone is preparing for his visit, joins in with the cleaning.

40 The Walking Stick: a Folk Tale for the Future. A story recounting the passing of the thirteenth Dalai Lama and the search for his incarnation, the fourteenth Dalai Lama.

41 Crossing to the Other Side. A young monk realises he cannot return to his home monastery because the river has swollen, and the ford is too deep. He sees one of his teachers, sitting, reading on the monastery side of the swollen river and asks for guidance on how to cross the river.

THANKS

Many thanks go to Jane Metson and Yvonne Denton for their editing and constant encouragement.

Martyn Elton, for his editing, encouragement and being there through these difficult times.

Daisy Dog for always laying at my feet whilst I work.

The History Press for trusting me.

References and Further Reading

Kundun: Biography of the Family of the Dalai Lama, by Mary Craig (HarperCollins Publishers, London, 1998)

The Dhammapada: The Sayings of The Buddha, by Thomas Byrom (Ebury Publishing, Random House, London, 2002)

The Illustrated Encyclopaedia of Buddhist Wisdom, by Gill Farrer-Halls (designed for Godsfield Press by The Bridgewater Book Company, 2000)

The Jātaka (or *Stories of the Buddha's Former Births*), by Edward Byles Cowell, H.T. Francis, Robert Alexander Neil and W.H.D. Rouse, translated by Robert Chalmers, B.A. Bristol, Pali Text Society, original edition in 6 volumes, 1895–1907

The Life of the Buddha, by Rev. Siridhamma (Buddhist Cultural Centre, Sri Lanka, 2006)

Wisdom Tales from Around the World, by Heather Forest (August House, Arkansas

Websites

himalayanart.org
spiritualgrowthevents.com/tag/spiritual-story
buddhistelibrary.org

The destination for history
www.thehistorypress.co.uk